THIS IS THE STORY of the world's most famous physicist as it has never been told before. In the opening pages we are privy to a conversation that Einstein had with a young woman at the very end of his life. It's a conversation that wasn't meant to happen, but it set off a chain of events that resulted in *Albert Einstein Speaking*.

ALBERT EINSTEIN SPEAKING

ALBERT EINSTEIN SPEAKING

R.J. Gadney

CANONGATE

Published in Great Britain in 2018 by Canongate Books Ltd,
14 High Street, Edinburgh EH1 1TE

canongate.co.uk

1

Copyright © R.J. Gadney, 2018

The moral right of the author has been asserted

All quotations from the works and correspondence of Albert Einstein © The Hebrew
University of Jerusalem

The author and publisher would like to thank The Albert Einstein Archives and The
Hebrew University of Jerusalem for their help and support of this publication

Further information on copyright material within the text is given on p.259

British Library Cataloguing-in-Publication Data
A catalogue record for this book is available on
request from the British Library

ISBN 978 1 78689 047 4

Typeset in Utopia by Palimpsest Book Production Ltd,
Falkirk, Stirlingshire

Printed and bound in the USA

Nell, Jago, Toby, Elliot
&
Tom

'If everybody lived a life like mine
there would be no need for novels.'

Albert Einstein, aged twenty, to his sister, Maja, 1899

▸▸▸▸◂ ONE ▸▸▸▸◂

Princeton, New Jersey,

14 March 1954

'Albert Einstein speaking.'

'Who?' asks the girl on the telephone.

It's the morning of Albert's seventy-fifth birthday. He's seated at his study table on the second floor of his small house on Mercer Street in Princeton turning the pages of his scrapbook embossed in silver:

ALBERT EINSTEIN SAMMELALBUM

He presses the black plastic Western Electric telephone closer against his ear.

'I'm sorry,' the girl says. 'I have the wrong number.' Her accent is Boston Brahmin.

'You have the right number,' Albert says.

'I do? May I ask, sir, please – what is your number?'

'I don't know—'

'You don't know your own phone number? You are Albert

Einstein. How come the world's most famous scientist doesn't know his own phone number?'

'Never memorise something that you can look up,' Albert says. 'Or, even better, have someone else look up for you.'

Tobacco sparks from his briar pipe spew across a letter from the German physicist Max Born. Albert extinguishes them with a slap.

'OK, sir,' the girl says. 'I'm sorry I bothered you.'

'You haven't bothered me in the least. How old are you?'

'Seventeen.'

'I'm seventy-five today.'

'You are? Seventy-five – that's something. Happy birthday.'

'Thank you. You have given me a fine birthday present.'

'I have?'

'You have raised an interesting philosophical problem. You dialled a wrong number. The wrong number for you. The right number for me. It is a most intriguing conundrum. What is your name?'

'Mimi Beaufort—'

'Where are you calling from?'

'From my lodgings, outside Princeton.'

'Your lodgings, you say – where's your real home?'

'Greenwich in Fairfield County, Connecticut.'

'That's a nice place. Will you call me again?'

'If you really are Albert Einstein, I'll call again. Sure I will.'

Albert toys with his copious white moustache. 'Check me out in the directory.'

His right leg is jiggling and bouncing. The ball of his foot rises and lowers rapidly. He flexes his calf muscles. He's quite unaware his leg is making such rapid movements.

*

Puffing at his pipe, filled with Revelation, a tobacco blended by Philip Morris and House of Windsor, Albert gazes at the birthday cards and cables piled up on the desk and tables, even on his wooden music stand. He hasn't the foggiest idea who's sent them.

There are congratulatory cables from people he does know: Jawaharlal Nehru, Thomas Mann, Bertrand Russell and Linus Pauling.

He shifts uneasily in his chair, troubled by the pain in his liver.

He opens *The New York Times* to find that its editorial page has quoted George Bernard Shaw's view that history would remember Albert's name as the equal of Pythagoras, Aristotle, Galileo and Newton.

On chairs, mahogany commodes and occasional tables are mimeographed academic papers from Princeton University's Institute for Advanced Study marked for his personal attention: papers from mathematicians, physicists, archaeologists, astronomers and economists. A rack of briar pipes stands next to jars of pencils in front of a gramophone and vinyl records, mostly of violin and piano music by Bach and Mozart.

There are four portraits on the wall. One of Isaac Newton. A second of James Maxwell whose work Albert has described as the most profound and the most fruitful that physics has experienced since the time of Newton. A third of Michael Faraday. The fourth of Mahatma Gandhi. Beneath the portraits is the framed emblem of the Jain religion, symbol of the doctrine of non-violence. He looks at the letter from Born.

'I believe,' Born declares, 'that ideas such as absolute certitude, absolute exactness, final truth, etc. are figments of the imagination which should not be admissible in any field of science.'

'I agree,' says Albert to himself.

'On the other hand,' Born continues, 'any assertion of probability is either right or wrong from the standpoint of the theory on which it is based. This loosening of thinking [*Lockerung des Denkens*] seems

3

to me to be the greatest blessing which modern science has given to us.'

'Very good,' Albert mutters.

'For the belief in a single truth and in being the possessor thereof is the root cause of all evil in the world.'

'So says Born,' says Albert. 'Quite right.'

Albert's treasured Biedermeier-style grandfather clock chimes ten. When the chimes end, he smiles to himself. $F = L + S$. *Frieden entspricht Liebe und Stille*. Or: $P = L + S$. Peace equals Love plus Silence.

EINSTEIN ATTENDS A CONCERT WITH HELEN DUKAS AT THE GREAT SYNAGOGUE IN BERLIN, 1930

Outside Albert's study, his live-in secretary and housekeeper, Frau Helen Dukas, has been waiting until the clock chimes the hour. She doesn't like what she's just heard Albert saying on the telephone. 'You will call me again?'

You = another time-wasting female admirer.

She comes into the study bringing with her the aroma of camphor. Albert has long meant to tell her: 'The organic chemical

$C_{10}H_{16}O$ is unpleasant.' He's never quite summoned up the courage to do so.

Frau Dukas opens the green shutters of the study's main window with a flourish, the clatter intended as a reprimand. The window looks out onto the weeping willows, maples and elms of the leafy suburban street.

The sunlight increases the wateriness in Albert's eyes. He rubs them with the back of his hand and blinks.

Frau Dukas, austere, tall and slender, is originally from south-west Germany, the daughter of a German-Jewish merchant. Her mother was from Hechingen, the same town as Albert's second wife. As Albert's secretary and gatekeeper for some twenty-five years she's dedicated herself to providing him with a quiet life.

Her bedroom in the house on Mercer Street, separated by a bathroom, is next to Albert's. There's also a small studio and bedroom set aside for Albert's stepdaughter, Margot, when she visits. And another that had been Albert's sister, Maja's. Maja died four years ago.

'Who was that you were speaking to?' Frau Dukas asks.

'A young lady called Mimi Beaufort. I like her voice. From good old Boston. The home of the bean and the cod, where the Lowells talk only to Cabots and presumably the Beauforts. Families that talk only to God. D'you think you can find out who she is?'

'She calls you by mistake and you want me to find out who she is?'

'I do. Anyone who's never made a mistake has never tried anything new.'

'Do you mind me saying you mustn't waste your time?'

'Helen. *Kreativität ist das Resultat Verschwendeter Zeit.* Creativity is the residue of time wasted. Find out who this Mimi Beaufort is. Check out the name in the Greenwich, Connecticut, telephone directory. And please bring me a cup of hot chocolate.'

Albert wears scuffed leather slippers, no socks. His frayed shirt, open at the neck, reveals a worn blue sweatshirt.

Frau Dukas arranges a blanket around his feet. 'I have never seen so many birthday cards,' she marvels.

'What is there to celebrate? Birthdays are automatic things. Anyway, birthdays are for children.' Once again he wipes away the wateriness from his eyes. Their sparkle contrasts with the lines and furrows of his brow. 'I am seventy-five. None of us is getting any younger.'

He fills his pipe from the tin of Revelation tobacco and lights up. A cloud of smoke billows upwards. 'Please, Helen, bring me my hot chocolate.'

'All in good time.'

'What are you holding, Helen?'

Frau Dukas hands him a newspaper photograph of the mushroom cloud of the atomic bomb that destroyed Hiroshima on 6 August 1945.

'Some schoolchildren from Lincoln, Nebraska, have asked you to sign this. Are you prepared to sign it for them?'

Shrouded in the cloud of pipe smoke, Albert stares forlornly at the image. 'If I must.'

'I will get your cup of chocolate,' Frau Dukas says, as if promising a reward.

She leaves him alone to sign the photograph *A. Einstein 14 March 1954.*

Then he takes out a sheet of paper and writes:

140,000 souls perished at Hiroshima. 100,00 were terribly injured. 74,000 perished at Nagasaki. Another 75,000 suffered fatal injuries from burns, injuries, and gamma radiation. At Pearl Harbor – how many died? They tell me 2,500. The British poet Donne tells us:

'any man's death diminishes me, because I am involved in mankind; and therefore never send to know for whom the bell tolls; it tolls for thee.' The western world is satisfied, satisfied. I am not. The wonderful things you learn in school are the work of many generations, produced by enthusiastic effort and infinite labor in every country of the world. All this is put into your hands as your inheritance in order that you may receive it, honor it, add to it, and one day faithfully hand it to your children. Thus do we mortals achieve immortality in the permanent things that we create in common.

Frau Dukas returns with the hot chocolate. Albert loads more tobacco in his pipe, waving at Frau Dukas to be seated: 'A letter please . . . Helen, to Bertrand Russell.' He dictates: 'I agree with your draft proposition that the prospect for the human race is sombre beyond all precedent. Mankind is faced with a clear-cut alternative: either we shall all perish, or we shall have to acquire some slight degree of common sense.'

The grandfather clock chimes the quarter hour. 'Here, then, is the problem,' Albert continues, 'which we present to you, stark and dreadful and inescapable: Shall we put an end to the human race; or shall mankind renounce war? People will not face this alternative because it is so difficult to abolish war – With kind regards, Albert Einstein.'

He takes off one of his old slippers, removes a small granite pebble from between his toes and sets it on top of Born's letter.

'I liked the young lady's voice. Think of relativity. When a man sits with a pretty girl for an hour, it seems like a minute. But let him sit on a hot stove for a minute – and it's longer than any hour. That's relativity. Mimi Beaufort. Beaufort is a remarkable name.'

'Why?' Frau Dukas says with a tone that suggests there's nothing remarkable about it.

Turning towards the windows to ponder the play of dappled sunlight on the trees, Albert says: 'It means the beautiful fortress.'

The sight of a group of Afro-American children playing in the sun makes him smile.

The leader sings: 'My momma livin . . .'

The group sings: 'Where she livin?'

Performing a hip-shaking dance, they sing in unison:

'Well, she lives in a place called Tennessee.

Jump up, Tenna, Tennessee.

Well, I never been to college,

I never been to school.

But when it comes to boogie

I can boogie like a fool.

You go in, out, side to side.

You go in, out, side to side.'

Albert struggles to his feet and performs a boogie-woogie of his own devising. Still with his back to Frau Dukas, he says: 'Take this down, please: "There remain prejudices of which I as a Jew am clearly conscious; but they are unimportant in comparison with the attitude of whites towards their fellow citizens of darker complexion. The more I feel an American, the more this situation pains me. I can escape the feeling of complicity in it only by speaking out."'

'Who is that to be sent to?' Frau Dukas asks.

'To me. To me, Helen. A reminder to myself. Now . . . I want you to treat the following as strictly confidential.' He sighs heavily. 'My personal relationships have all been failures. What man would not visit his stepdaughter when she was dying of cancer? My first wife died alone in Zürich. My daughter has disappeared. I have no idea where she is. I don't even know whether she is still alive.'

'Please . . . don't allow your past to destroy you.'

'My son – my son . . . you know, Helen – my son Eduard has been in clinics for schizophrenics for almost twenty-five years. Therapy, electroconvulsive treatment, has destroyed his memory and cognitive abilities.'

'But not your loving relationship with him.'

'My only loving relationship is with the Jewish people. That is my strongest human bond. I told Queen Elizabeth of Belgium: "The exaggerated esteem in which my lifework is held makes me very ill at ease. I feel compelled to think of myself as an involuntary swindler – *Ich bin ein Betrüger.*" I need fresh air – my liver hurts.'

Frau Dukas opens the windows.

Outside, from the radio of a battered Buick four-door sedan, comes the sound of Doris Day singing 'Secret Love'.

Albert makes a gesture of impatience. 'Check out that telephone directory, Helen.'

Frau Dukas does so and discovers the Beaufort family residence is Beaufort Park in Greenwich, Fairfield County, Connecticut. He wonders what Mimi Beaufort looks like. Her voice certainly holds the eternal appeal of youth. Is she going to be a new friend? A confidante perhaps. A secret love to calm his soul troubled by his age, his aches and pains and dark forebodings. The shafts of sun fall across his desk. He relishes the patterns. He flicks through the worn pages of Mozart's Sonata for Piano and Violin in E minor, K.304.

It's an honour to find such tenderness unfolding, such purity of beauty and truth. Such qualities are indestructible. He believes, like Mozart, he has unravelled the complexities of the universe. Its essence of the eternal is beyond fate's hand and deluded humankind. Age allows us to feel such things.

He stares at the shadows flickering on the floor. In the patterns he fancies he sees the faces of his family, his friends and loved ones.

His intimate and treasured friendships seem to him to have been cyclical. Too many have evaporated. Ever since his beginning. Long ago. In Ulm at eleven-thirty in the morning at Bahnhofstrasse B135, the house destroyed by one of the most violent Allied air attacks in December 1944. He remembers writing to a correspondent whose name he's forgotten: 'Time has affected it even more than it has affected me.'

Is there anything left now of old Ulm? he wonders. What of my friends and loved ones: those who have made up my life and formed me? Me: The Most Famous Face on Earth.

How kind to me were the residents of Ulm who intended to name a street after me. Instead, the Nazis named it Fichtestrasse after Fichte, whose works Hitler read, and who was read by other Nazis like Dietrich Eckart and Arnold Fanck.

After the war, it was renamed Einsteinstrasse. His response to the news sent to him by the mayor always makes him smile. 'There's a street there that bears my name. At least I'm not responsible for whatever is going to happen there. I was right to decline the rights of a freeman of Ulm considering the fate of the Jews in Nazi-Germany.'

He takes up his pen and writes:

Like you I cannot help my birthplace. But I can help my history of my intimacies in youth. The religious paradise of youth was my first attempt to free myself from the chains of the 'merely personal', from an existence dominated by wishes, hopes, and primitive feelings. Out yonder there is the world in all its vastness existing independently of us human beings standing before us like a great, eternal riddle, at least partially accessible to our inspection and thinking. The contemplation of this world beckons as a liberation. In childhood I noticed that many a man whom I had learned to esteem and to admire had found inner freedom and security in its pursuit. The mental grasp of this extra-personal world within the frame of our capabilities presented itself to my mind, half consciously, half unconsciously, as a supreme goal. Similarly motivated men of the present and of the past, as well as the insights they had achieved, were the friends who could not be lost. The road to this paradise was not as comfortable and alluring as the road to the religious paradise; but it has shown itself reliable, and I have never regretted having chosen it. Except perhaps for the fact I doubt there is a sentient being anywhere on earth who does not know my face.

►►►◄ TWO ►►►◄

Ulm, Württemberg, Germany

HERE IS MY FATHER, HERMANN;
AND MY MOTHER, PAULINE

'The head, the head,' the twenty-one-year-old Pauline Einstein cries.
'It's monstrous.'

'It's a beautiful head,' says Hermann Einstein squinting through
his pince-nez balanced precariously on his nose above his walrus moustache. 'Our son, Abraham, has a beautiful head.'

'It's deformed.'

13

'Abraham is not deformed, Pauline.'

'The skull, look at it, Hermann.'

'It's fine.'

'It is not fine. It's at a twisted angle to the rest of him.'

The couple fall silent. Only the sounds from the city break the silence.

Ulm is a noisy Swabian city in southwest Germany on the River Danube famed for the 531-foot spire of its minster, *der Fingerzeig Gottes*, the Finger of God, the tallest in the world. Mozart played its organ in 1763.

Horses, coal carts and small whistling steam engines fill its narrow winding cobbled streets lined with half-timbered houses. The stench of warm horse dung is overpowering.

The Einstein residence on Bahnhofstrasse is a stone's throw from the train station. *Der Blitzzug*, the lightning Paris–Istanbul express, has begun making scheduled stops at Ulm.

Hermann Einstein toys with his moustache. Then he glances at his hair in the mirror, gently patting it in place.

'I have been thinking about the child's name. Our family belongs to the Jewish community. I want a name that means noble and intelligent.'

'Which is what?'

'Albert. Albert Einstein.'

On 15 March 1879, the day after Albert's birth, a hackney cab takes mother, father and tiny son through the fog to the office of Ulm's registrar of births. Hermann, in the fine tailored black suit with a narrow necktie tied in a bow that befits a former partner in the featherbed manufacturers Israel & Levi, stands proudly before the registrar with Pauline, who carries baby Albert. Pauline's exuberant finery consists of a ribboned bonnet, a boned bodice, and matching skirt in folds, drapes and pleats.

The parents appear a prosperous couple. The featherbed

company may have failed two years ago, but now Hermann has decided to go into business with his younger brother, Jakob.

Jakob has a college degree in engineering and realises that electrification is the coming thing. Hermann's commercial savvy will be of value. More to the point though, Pauline's father is a wealthy grain dealer and well connected in Württemberg. With any luck Hermann will be able to get substantial funds from his in-laws to establish Elektrotechnische Fabrik J. Einstein & Cie, manufacturing electrical equipment and based in Munich.

The registrar of births reads aloud: 'No 224. Ulm, March 15, 1879. Today, the merchant Hermann Einstein, residing in Ulm, Bahnhofstrasse 135, of the Israelitic faith, personally known, appeared before the under-signed registrar, and stated that a male child, who has received the name Albert, was born in Ulm, in his residence, to his wife Pauline Koch, of the Israelitic faith, on March 14 of the year 1879, at 11.30 a.m. Read, confirmed, and signed: Hermann Einstein. The Registrar, Hartmann.'

Now it's official.

The registrar gives the child a look of practised admiration. Pauline at once covers the enormity of the head. She feels guilty and angry for having produced such a strange creature.

Back home the doctor calls later that afternoon.

Pauline whispers. 'The head, the head. Albert is unnatural.'

'I wouldn't go as far as to say that,' the doctor says. 'The large cranium could simply be a reflection of a larger-than-average-headed mother or father. It isn't an indication of a learning disorder or disability. Mind you, a large head can be linked to problems within the skull. We will measure Albert's head and make sure the circumference has been increasing since birth. I can reassure you of one thing. I see no compli-cations. Albert will be possessed of normal intelligence.'

'Normal intelligence?'

'Yes. Normal intelligence.'

Pauline watches Albert grow and, other than to Hermann, keeps her misgivings about him to herself and prays to Almighty God that she hasn't given birth to *eine Laune der Natur*: a freak of nature.

AGED TWO, OR THEREABOUTS

'A new toy for me, a new toy for me,' Albert exclaims when he first sees his little sister Maria, familiarly known as Maja, on 18 November 1881. 'Where are the wheels?'

Once settled in Munich, first in a rented house, Müllerstrasse 3, later at Rengerweg 14 with a spacious garden, the Einsteins enjoy a bourgeois existence.

'Albert is slow to talk like other children,' Pauline says to Fanny, her visiting older sister. 'Why does he say everything twice?'

Pauline embroiders a tablecloth with the words *Sich regen bringt Segen* – Hard work brings its own reward.

'A new toy for me,' Albert says again slowly. 'Where are the wheels?'

'See what I mean, Fanny?'

'Maybe he's just curious.'

'Curious. Curious. I don't want a child who's curious. I want a child who's normal.'

'It'll be a shame if he only hears you being so critical. He'll retreat inside himself. You won't know who he is.'

'I know who he is. If he goes on like this he'll never amount to anything.'

'Does anyone else think the same as you?'

'Of course. Even the housekeeper says that Albert is a *schwachkopf* [dimwit]. The child mutters to himself.'

Albert stares at his mother then at his aunt and smiles. He moves his lips. Grunts. Salivates. Forms an incomprehensible phrase.

'What is it you're trying to say, Albert?' his mother asks.

Saliva dribbles from Albert's lips. He stamps his left foot.

'Don't dribble!' his mother snaps. 'Look, Fanny. He's quite unlike other children. The housekeeper's right.'

He clambers to his feet. He thinks before taking each step, holding out his pudgy arms to steady himself. 'The earth is shaking beneath my feet. *Ein Erdbeben.* An earthquake. *Wunderschön!*'

'Play the piano,' Fanny says to Pauline. 'You told me in your letter he likes it when you play the piano.'

Pauline goes to the piano and Albert waddles across the carpet to her side.

Pauline plays Mozart.

Albert watches captivated as Pauline plays Mozart's Piano

17

Sonata in C minor, K.457. 'Don't stop, Mama. Go on, go on.'

'I can't spend the rest of my life playing the piano for him,' Pauline says.

'Maybe he'll become a pianist,' Fanny says.

The same evening, his father embarks upon readings from Schiller.

Albert nestles in his lap listening intently, entranced by the sound of his father's voice. '"There is no such thing as chance; and what seems to us merest accident springs from the deepest source of destiny." ... "Only those who have the patience to do simple things perfectly will acquire the skill to do difficult things easily." ... "Man only plays when in the full meaning of the word he is a man, and he is only completely a man when he plays."'

From Heine: '"Wherever they burn books they will also, in the end, burn human beings."'

And: '"Every period of time is a sphinx that throws itself into the abyss as soon as its riddle has been solved."'

And: '"The Romans would never have found time to conquer the world if they had been obliged first to learn Latin."'

Albert gives his father a smile of admiration.

Members of the Einstein and Koch families frequently beat a path to Rengerweg 14 from across Germany and northern Italy.

Rowdy children fill the garden at the back of Rengerweg 14, including Albert's cousins Elsa, Paula and Hermine, the daughters of Fanny. Fanny's married to Rudolf Einstein, a textile manufacturer from Hechingen. Rudolf is the son of Hermann Einstein's uncle, Rafael. The families relish the complexity of these byzantine relationships. Young Albert memorises all their names.

Increasingly, he prefers to keep his own company. His body and his mind seem separated. A woman visitor suggests he's isolated like no other boy. He opens his brown eyes wide. Observers notice they are dark and lustreless, like the eyes of a sightless child.

He stays on the sidelines observing pigeons or manoeuvring his toy sailing boat in a water bucket. He shies away from competitive sport or games of any sort; just mooches about alone, sometimes in a temper, or shuts himself away playing with a steam engine, a gift from his maternal uncle, Caesar Koch, in Brussels, a stationary model mimicking a factory, or a mobile engine such as those used in steam locomotives and boats. It has spring safety valves and whistles. The house is filled with the sound of chuffing, crank noises and the endless steam whistles.

Albert delights in irritating the family with the noise of the steam engine. 'Choo-choo!' he shouts. 'Clackety-clack. Tuff tuff tuff, *die Eisenbahn!*'

He watches them from the corners of his eyes.

To Albert's disappointment influenza means that he will have to spend his fifth birthday in bed.

'Look what I've got for you,' his father announces. 'Here—'

He hands Albert a small package.

'May I open it, Papa?'

'Of course.'

'Are you going to tell me what it is?'

'Discover for yourself.'

Albert opens the wrapping paper, then a small box, and takes out a compass.

'Papa. This is wonderful. Thank you from the bottom of my heart. Thank you.'

'I hope you like it.'

'I love it, Papa.'

Albert strokes the small glass window of the compass.

'Good. I'll see you again later.'

'I love you, Papa.'

'I love you too, Albert.'

Once alone, Albert turns and shakes the device, certain he can fool it into pointing its needle in a direction of his own devising. Yet the needle always finds its way back to point in the direction of magnetic north.

In turn enchanted and pleasurably scared by the miracle, his hands shake and his whole body grows cold. The force is invisible: proof that the world is possessed of hidden mysterious powers. There's something behind things, something deeply hidden.

Maja watches her seven-year-old brother in wonder as he builds a house of playing cards fourteen storeys high.

'It is a miracle,' she says. 'How do you do it?'

'It is scientific engineering,' Albert tells her. When he is interested in something or someone he speaks fluently. 'Watch, Maja. I use old cards. See? First I create the highest point. I put a pair of cards against each other in the shape of a triangle. I make a line of them. Now I build two apexes. I select a card to be the roof piece and place it above the two apexes. I hold it and lower it carefully till it's just above them. With the roof piece on I adjust the cards gently. I take my roofed apexes and make a third apex, then a fourth and now a fifth and on and on.'

'Albert, it's a miracle. Will you perform miracles and lead your life like Jesus in the Bible?'

'Maja. We are instructed in the Bible and the Talmud. We are Jews. We are Jews.'

'What d'you think about Jesus? You know so much.'

'I know nothing.'

'But you know everything.'

'No, Maja. The more I learn, the more I realise how much I don't know.'

His curiosity constantly gets the better of him.

He wanders aimlessly through the neighbourhood, market-places and covered passages, careful to avoid the heavy brewers' drays jolting and rumbling past. Pauline, to Albert's pleasure, encourages his explorations. She begins to allow him greater freedom. To think, to be alone with his convictions.

He watches students playing *Kegel* or ninepins in the drizzle.

'Please may I have a go?' Albert asks.

'You may have a go, little man,' a student laughs. 'Here.' He rolls the ball to Albert.

But the ball is too hefty for Albert and he altogether misses the ninepins. Then falls over.

The students laugh at him. Albert tries to hide the pain of being the butt of the students' humour.

He walks home in tears.

To cheer him up, his father takes him out in a *Droschke*, the latest hackney cab, a new feature of Munich transport. They rattle through the Isartor, the eastern gate separating the old town from the districts of Isarvorstadt and Lehel, his father pointing out the frescos of the victory procession of Emperor Ludwig of Bavaria.

A woman tutor is called upon to teach Albert, who sees her appointment as a useless interruption to his thinking.

He throws a chair at her. Terrified, she at once clears off never to be seen again. Albert simply wants to be left alone sitting quietly, reading, with no one paying attention to him.

His thirst for knowledge is unquenchable. It takes him on solitary journeys of the mind to places where no one else can follow. Here he is happiest. And he continues his amblings around Munich.

On one walk in the driving sleet an elderly Italian offers the bedraggled Albert shelter in his grand house.

Albert stares at the glass cabinets filled with knick-knacks of glass, china and small models. Standing on a satinwood table is a model of Milan Cathedral built of cream-coloured cardboard. The tracery of the windows, the bas-reliefs, columns, pinnacles and statues are made of bread. The old man is not an architect. He says he's built his models from his imagination. 'I spend my life in my head,' the old man says.

'So do I,' says Albert. 'What is the grave?'

'The model of my wife's grave. She died two years ago in bed. Where the model's standing. The model marks the place of death.'

Albert tells his father about the kindly Italian. Hermann says: 'The signore is entirely self-educated. He made a small fortune in his twenties and with nothing much to do he lives with his models in his imagination.'

As a special treat Hermann takes Albert to watch the first voyage of the small steamer on Lake Starnberg on the morning of the Frühlingsfestival, the spring festival. At the time steamboats are more common on the Danube, Elbe and Rhine.

It's a beautiful day. Albert savours the fragrances of white viburnams and narcissi. In the meadows he identifies the lilac flowers of *Crocus tommasinianus*.

It seems all Munich has turned out on the banks of Lake Starnberg among the beech woods. The white Starnberg houses, St Joseph's church and the hotel built like a Swiss chalet captivate Albert. Far in the distance he can see the Alps. Blue. Silver. Rose-blue. Jagged peaks. Pale orange.

In the foreground, flags, wreaths and drapery decorate the houses. Albert watches the steamer being decorated with garlands. At the edge of the woods, for his mother and Maja, he assembles bouquets of Alpine gentians and oxlips. No matter that the midday meal is of rubbery boiled beef and a dry potato salad. Albert and his father join in the merrymaking as the boat is launched.

By night, he has difficulty sleeping. Mainly because he's frightened of the dark. He lies awake waiting until he hears his father and mother go to bed, when it's safe to tiptoe barefoot out of his room and light the *Stubenlampe*. The thin wick is wide, providing a comforting circle of white-reddish light. Back in bed he gazes at the light coming through the slit at the bottom of the door. It banishes the idea of a prowling monster born after a suicide or sometimes an accidental death. It heralds sickness, disease, agony and oblivion. Finally, it eats its family members, then devours its own body and funeral shrouds.

At dawn he wakes, restless. The light beneath the door is now a hindrance to sleeping. Anyway, he doesn't want his parents to know he turned it on. So he creeps out of his room again and turns it off.

Back in bed the light coming into his room through the gap in the wooden shutters bothers him. He buries his head in the pillow. But of course the light's still there. It's entered his room from 93 million miles away. Thank you, Sun.

Quick journey. Travelling at 186,000 miles per second. So that light, coming through the shutters, was in the Sun eight minutes ago. *I can slow it down.* He moves the glass of water towards the rays. The light rays bend, refract. He screws up his eyes. The light comes through his eyelashes and spreads out in stripes. Tighter, tighter, he screws up his eyes. The light spreads wider. When he completely closes his eyes it vanishes.

Each November, after several days of snowfall, to Albert's delight, sledging begins.

In the Englischer Garten, Albert marvels at the heavy snow hanging in strange shapes on the dark branches of the fir trees. The purity and silence is broken by the sound of bells from a bright green and gilded sledge drawn by a black horse. The rider is wrapped up in a cloak, with a fur cap over his brows.

Carriages on sledges instead of wheels fill the streets. Everything travels on sledges: tubs of water and buckets, wooden milk pails hooped with brass. Everyone takes a childish pleasure in the sledges. The colours of the winter enthral him. Red leaves, rose-green and silver leaves, the fantastical bowers of clematis festooning branches and the heaps of pure white snow. The light is dazzling. It sparkles and bends and bends.

'We'll go to the Aumeister,' his father announces.

'What's the Aumeister?'

'Best coffee in the city, pretty ladies and cakes. Lots of cakes. Mainly pretty ladies.'

'Pretty ladies, pretty ladies,' sings Albert.

He loves his father's gaiety.

Aged twelve he likes to hold forth on religion and culture at home.

His father delights in introducing Albert.

'I have the honour to ask Professor Einstein to address the family on a subject of his choice.'

'Thank you. Today the subject of my lecture is Ashkenazic or Ashkenazim Jews, with some modest proposals.'

The family applaud.

'As we all know, we are Ashkenazi Jews. The Ashkenazim came together as a distinct community of Jews in the Holy Roman Empire towards the end of the first millennium. According to *Halakha*, Shabbat is observed from a few minutes before sunset on Friday evening until the appearance of three stars in the sky on Saturday. The lighting of candles and the recitation of a blessing usher Shabbat in. The evening meal typically begins with our blessing, *kiddush*, proclaimed over two loaves of *challah*. Shabbat is closed the following evening with a *Havdalah*. On Shabbat we are free from the regular labours of life. We contemplate life's spirituality. We spend time with the family.

'I now turn to diet. My proposal is that we don't eat pork. Rather, matzo ball soup and pasta filled with chopped meat floating in broth, or corned beef with fried potato latkes, and slices of noodles mixed with dried fruit, fat and sugar.'

He suddenly falls silent.

'And?' says his mother.

'As we all know, we are Ashkenazi Jews. The Ashkenazim came together as a distinct community of Jews in the Holy Roman Empire towards the end of the first millennium.'

'Albert?' says his mother.

'Please don't interrupt, Mama.'

'But you've already said that.'

'It's the truth.'

'I cannot take this seriously,' says his mother.

'Anyone who doesn't take truth seriously in small matters cannot be trusted in large ones either.'

'I think we've heard enough,' she says.

I will never be understood, he tells himself.

'Algebra,' says Uncle Jakob, 'is the calculus of indolence. If you don't know a certain quantity, you call it x and treat it as if you do know it, then you put down the relationship given, and determine this x later.'

Uncle Jakob shows him the Pythagorean theorem and Albert hurls himself into solving it. It takes him only twenty-one days to reach the correct proof using his intellect and nothing else.

He sees the similarity of triangles by drawing a perpendicular from one vertex of the right-angled triangle onto the hypotenuse and leads to the proof he desperately seeks.

'There is no exclusively Jewish school in Munich,' Hermann tells his son. 'You will enter the Volksschule Petersschule on Blumenstrasse.'

'A nearby Catholic elementary school,' says Pauline.

'Not Jewish?' says Albert.

'Catholic,' says Pauline.

'Is this good news?' says Albert.

'It isn't bad news,' says Pauline.

Hermann keeps his own counsel.

Albert buries his head in *Struwwelpeter.* And memorises it.

> Just look at him! there he stands,
> With his nasty hair and hands.
> See! his nails are never cut;
> They are grimed as black as soot;
> And the sloven, I declare,
> Never once has combed his hair;
> Anything to me is sweeter
> Than to see Shock-headed Peter.

At first there's good news.

Pauline writes to her mother: 'Yesterday Albert got his school marks. He is at the top of his class and got a brilliant record.' And this is in spite of the ministrations of his teacher who teaches multiplication tables by beating the children whenever they make mistakes. Albert loathes the strict enforcement of obedience and discipline.

Nothing seems to deter him from mocking his conceited fellow pupils and self-opinionated teachers.

Of all his teachers, Albert gets on best with the instructor of religion. The teacher likes Albert. In this department all goes well until the teacher shows the children a large nail. He solemnly announces: 'This is the nail the Jews used to nail Jesus to the cross.'

The teacher's demonstration inflames the pupils' simmering anti-Semitism, which is at once directed straight at Albert.

They call him Honest John, lover of truth and justice. He counters the taunts with a twist of the mouth, a look of sarcasm, and sticks out his quivering lower lip. He learns, like many bullied schoolchildren then and now: the oxygen of schools, like society, is poisoned by power, perverted authority and fear – above all fear. The antidote is silence. Like his father, he learns to keep his own counsel.

The leader of the Jew-baiters spits at Albert.

'You are ostracised. You will not be talked to. You no longer exist. You are completely invisible and inaudible. Read Heinrich von Treitschke: "*Die Juden sind unser Unglück!* The Jews are our misfortune! The Jews are no longer necessary. The international Jew, hidden in the masks of different nationalities, is a disintegrating influence; he can be of no further use to the world." Neither are you. *Schmutzige Internationale Jude*. Dirty international Jew.'

Albert turns white. His hands shake. He feels the muscles tighten in his chest. Staring at his fellow pupils he sees all of them have turned their backs to him.

He hears himself say: 'There's scarcely a country in the world that doesn't have a Jewish segment in the population. Wherever Jews reside, they're a minority of the population, and a small minority at that, so they aren't powerful enough to defend themselves against attack. It's easy for governments to divert attention from their own mistakes by blaming Jews for this or that political theory, such as communism or socialism. Throughout history, Jews have been accused of all sorts of treachery, such as poisoning water wells or murdering children as religious sacrifices. Much of this can be attributed to jealousy, because,

27

despite the fact that Jewish people have always been thinly populated in various countries, they have always had a disproportionate number of outstanding public figures.'

The chant rises: '*Müll. Juden sind Perversen! Müll. Juden sind Perversen!*'

The other pupils beat their desks. '*Müll. Juden sind Perversen! Müll. Juden sind Perversen!*'

The schoolroom door opens.

'*Was ist hier los?*' [What's going on here?] the teacher yells above the din.

Albert pushes past him out of the Volksschule Petersschule.

He vows to be decisive. To take strength from the family. He hurries home, his dark felt hat covering his dark hair, walking fast as if in flight, with darting brown eyes and watchful, flickering stare. Singing *Struwwelpeter* to a tune of his own composition

HERE ARE MY FELLOW PUPILS AT THE LUITPOLD GYMNASIUM

I AM THIRD FROM THE RIGHT IN THE FRONT ROW

The year 1888 sees the founding of the National Geographic Society in the United States and the publication of Conan Doyle's *Valley of Fear* in the United Kingdom. In Braunau, 124 kilometres from Munich, Klara Hitler falls pregnant with her more notorious son. Likewise, Hannah Chaplin with Charlie in East Street, Walworth, south London. Meanwhile, Albert Einstein enters Munich's interdenominational Luitpold Gymnasium.

He enjoys the classes given by Heinrich Friedmann, shared with his Jewish classmates. Friedmann teaches the Ten Commandments and the Jewish holy-day rituals. Albert makes no bones about the school's disciplined study of Latin and Greek. He hates it.

'Books!' shouts the teacher. 'Pick up your books. *Struwwelpeter*. First page.'

Albert drops his on the floor.

'Leave it, Einstein!'

'What if I don't leave it?'

'Your knuckles will be thrashed.'

'Really, by whom?'

'By me.'

'I don't need the book.'

'You do need the book.'

'What happens if I know the first page?'

'You don't know it.'

'I do know it.'

'You are lying.'

'Do you know it?'

'You don't.'

The teacher is fast losing control of himself.

The other pupils begin to giggle.

'Quiet!' the teacher bawls. 'Einstein?'

Albert gives a theatrical sigh. 'If you insist.'

Albert recites *Struwwelpeter* in Latin:

The professor tells him: 'You're a fat little runt. You'll be no good for anything. You're a pathetic failure.'

'Perhaps I will achieve your remarkable status in a field of my own discovery,' Albert says with a smile.

'Get out! Go home. *Raus! Raus!*'

Shortly afterwards Albert begins work on theorems in earnest, at home, proving them for himself.

Max Talmud, an impoverished Polish student of medicine at the university in Munich, is a regular Thursday night dinner guest. Albert intrigues Max. Max gives him books. Albert devours Aaron Bernstein's *Naturwissenschaftlichen Volksbücher* (*Popular Books on Natural Science*) and Ludwig Büchner's *Kraft und Stoff* (*Force and Matter*). Bernstein and Büchner's works capture Albert's imagination, and Bernstein's books in particular vastly increase Albert's interest in physics.

Life in Munich changes abruptly when once more the Einstein business fails.

In 1894, when Albert is fifteen, the family elects to move to Milan because the Kochs feel they want a more direct influence on Hermann's business activity. Hermann and Pauline take Maja with them, depositing Albert in a boarding house.

'The plan,' Hermann says, 'is that you'll gain your diploma at the Luitpold Gymnasium and enter university and then pursue the profession of electrical engineer.' This, at any rate, is his father's plan. Albert has other ideas.

He sends a paper to his uncle Caesar in Stuttgart.

'I'm taking up the challenge of a highly disputed scientific subject,' he tells his uncle. 'This is the relationship between electricity, magnetism and the ether, the latter being the hypothetical entity that is non-material and believed to fill all of space and transmits electromagnetic waves.'

He writes out his thoughts in his thin Gothic script on five pages of lined paper. He entitles his study: 'Über die Untersuchung des Ätherzustandes im magnetischen Felde': 'On the Investigation of the State of Ether in Magnetic Fields'.

'Little is presently known about the relationship of magnetic fields with the ether,' the fifteen-year-old points out. 'But if the potential states of the ether in magnetic fields were to be examined in thorough experimental studies then the absolute magnitude of the ether, of its elastic force and density, might be begun.'

The boy has discovered an extraordinary paradox.

'What might happen if you follow a light beam at the same speed as light travels? The result is a spatially oscillatory electromagnetic field at rest.'

He adds that 'it is still rather naive and imperfect, as is to be expected from a young fellow like myself. I shall not mind if you don't bother to read the stuff; but you must recognise it at least as a modest attempt to overcome the laziness in writing which I have inherited from both my dear parents.'

Albert has three more years to complete his studies at the Gymnasium before university.

He's left behind to lodge with a relative and sinks into a depression. He turns to the family doctor and confesses he's suffering from a serious nervous malaise.

Matters take a strange twist. Albert's professor of Greek, Degenhart, tells him to leave the Gymnasium. Simple as that.

'What've I done wrong?' Albert pleads.

'You're a disruptive influence,' the professor says.

'Of course I'm disruptive. I don't approve of your educational methods.'

'Then leave.'

31

'You don't want to hear my arguments?'

'I do not.'

'Your reluctance makes my point.'

He packs his things and follows the rest of the family to Milan.

The lack of a really settled formal education secretly suits Albert. Simply, it leaves him to his own devices, immersed in thought. He is someone apart: single-minded. In one essay, 'Mes Projets d'Avenir' ('My Plans for the Future'), he confesses he has no 'practical talent'. Yet, 'There is a certain independence in the profession of science that greatly appeals to me.'

He can't accept the German soul, as it seems to be embodied by the likes of Degenhart. *Of course I'm disruptive.*

Worse still, Germans are required to undertake military service. There's one way out. *Get out of the country well before my seventeenth birthday and renounce my citizenship. Otherwise I'll be arrested for desertion.*

He takes the train to Pavia, thirty-five kilometres south of Milan, where his parents will have no alternative but to welcome him.

He loves travelling on the *Schnellzug*: the express train. He listens to the sound of the slamming doors heralding departure. He savours the smell of coal-generated steam, the engines panting, screaming whistles. The clackety-clack, diddley-dum, diddley-dum of the wheels on the wrought-iron rails. The dancing sparks of burning grit. The driven rain coursing down the windows. The sight of the enormous Munich marshalling yards and Hagans Bn2t locomotives. Slag heaps. In winter: blackened snow, barns and old lime trees. In spring: orchards in bloom. In high summer: cornfields like silver, Alpine pastures, trees of pine, golden harvest hay. Over the points. His journeys alone afford him time to think without interruption. He shuts his ears to the gabble of fellow passengers, lost in the ideas swirling around in his brain to the rhythm of the train.

Meine Gedankenexperimente. My thought experiments.

On the journey to Pavia he reads Mozart's letter to his father: 'A fellow of mediocre talent will remain a mediocrity, whether he travels or not; but one of superior talent (which without impiety I cannot deny that I possess) will go to seed if he always remains in the same place.'

I must not remain in the same place.

THE WORKSHOP OF ELEKTROTECHNISCHE FABRIK J. EINSTEIN & CO., PAVIA, 1894

The Einsteins exhibit dynamos, lamps, and even a telephone system at the first international electro-technical exhibition in Frankfurt. The Einstein firm is issued with several patents.

Now called the Elektrotechnische Fabrik J. Einstein & Co., the firm employs 200 people and starts installing lighting and power networks and is awarded the contract to install the electric lighting for the Oktoberfest. Then the firm wires Schwabing in northern Munich. Jakob's dynamos are shown at the International Electrical

Exhibition in Frankfurt, generating 100 horsepower, 75,000 watts. A million people, along with the Kaiser, marvel at the lights. They gain contracts to instal power in the northern Italian towns of Varese and Susa.

Unfortunately, upwards of a million marks is needed to compete in the burgeoning market for power plants. The Einsteins face massive competition from Deutsche Edison-Gesellschaft and Siemens.

In desperation they mortgage their home. The capital is insufficient. Schuckert of Nuremberg gains the contract. Within twelve months Elektrotechnische Fabrik J. Einstein & Co. is broke.

'The misfortune of my poor parents,' Albert confides in Maja, 'who for so many years have not had a happy moment, weighs most heavily on me. It also hurts me deeply that at sixteen I must be a passive witness without being able to do even the smallest thing about it. I am nothing but a burden to my relatives. It would surely be better if I did not live at all. Only the thought that year after year I do not allow myself a pleasure, a diversion, keeps me going and must protect me often from despair.'

The brothers Einstein turn to northern Italy. They sell the house in Munich and look to constructing a hydroelectric power system for Pavia. Once there they make a new home in a grand house that had belonged to the poet Ugo Foscolo.

Albert falls in love with Italy. He assists his father and uncle with designs, reads, thinks, hikes alone across the Ligurian Alps to Genoa, where he stays with his uncle Jakob Koch.

He spends the summer of 1895 in Airolo writing essays and philosophical notes inspired by Leibniz: 'It is wrong to infer from the imperfection of our thinking that objects are imperfect.'

'You'll have to earn a living,' his father tells him. 'Take up electrical engineering in preparation to take on the Einstein business.'

'No, Father. I'll take the entrance exams for the Eidgenössische Technische Hochschule in Zürich.'

'It's only a teacher-training college. Not a university like Heidelberg, Berlin or Göttingen.'

'It'll do.'

Hermann makes an official application for Albert to be relieved of his citizenship in the state of Württemberg, which is accepted, costing three marks. It excuses him from military service. No more a German citizen, he'll be a stateless student at the ETH.

Not quite. The director of the ETH is unenthusiastic about Albert's application. He hasn't got entirely the right qualifications and has only achieved the Matura, the high-school diploma. The director announces: 'According to my experience it is not advisable to withdraw a student from the institution in which he had begun his studies even if he is a so-called child prodigy.' Albert should finish his general studies. Even so, if the Einsteins insist, the director will make an exception in so far as the age rule is concerned and allow Albert to sit the entrance exam, which Albert does.

Alas, he does so badly in languages and history that he is sent back for another year in secondary school, thirty minutes from Zürich in Aarau, in the canton of Aargau. The Aarau Kantonsschule has a fairly liberal reputation and specialises in science.

AARAU

35

At the start of the autumn term Albert goes to Aarau, forty-five kilometres from Zürich, where arrangements are made for him to be housed with the Winteler family. Jost Winteler teaches philology and history at the Kantonsschule.

The sixteen-year-old Albert feels at ease in the Winteler house, thinking of them as his second family. Jost Winteler, a native of Switzerland's Toggenburg region, is a former journalist and an ornithologist. A handsome, free-thinking liberal, he loathes power politics, and he and Albert share a profound disapproval of German militarism. The Wintelers have four sons and three daughters. The house is filled with books, music, parties and spirited discussion. Winteler arranges kite-flying excursions. He has a habit of chatting with his birds. For the country treks Albert sports his grey felt hat.

The family treats the young smiling philosopher as one of its own. Albert calls Jost Winteler 'Papa' and his wife, Pauline, 'Mamerl' or 'Mummy No. 2'. He treats Mamerl as his confessor.

He spends hours hanging around in his blue nightshirt drinking coffee with one of the sons of the house, Paul, who becomes his close friend. Albert relishes his reputation as a subversive student. He entrances the women of the household, captivating them with his bright eyes, bedraggled hair and insolent expressions. He plays Bach and Mozart for them on his violin. His playing is powerful and graceful. Eighteen-year-old Marie, who accompanies him on the piano, is a pupil at the Aargau teachers' college. In her long full skirt and blouse with flared sleeves, she is the most beautiful of the three daughters. Albert feels powerfully attracted to her. Playfully, he quotes Goethe's 'The Ratcatcher' to her: 'I bid the chords sweet music make, And all must follow in my wake.'

No matter that Marie is far from his intellectual equal, the couple fall in love. They laugh and are rarely out of each other's sight. They meet with friends at one or other *Kaffeehaus*.

The families have no objection; indeed, they treat the pair as unofficially engaged. When Albert returns to Pavia on a spring holiday, Marie's letters, he admits to his mother, allow him to understand home-sickness. He writes to Marie: 'Dear little sunshine, You mean more to my soul than the whole world did before.'

MARIE'S FAVOURITE PHOTOGRAPH

She calls him *Geliebter Schatz*: Beloved Treasure.

In his letters to her from Pavia, Albert's realistic about the love affair. She admits she can't keep up with his thinking. Albert is obsessed with the nature of electromagnetism. He fantasises about what he might see riding along on a light wave. Marie finds it unromantic.

He has Berlin in his sights, where he's heard that Wilhelm Röntgen has made advanced studies into cathode radiation. The radiation occurs when an electrical charge is applied to two metal plates inside a glass tube filled with low-density gas. Röntgen sees a faint glow on light-sensitive screens: a penetrating, previously unknown type of radiation causes it, X-ray radiation.

The obstacle to Albert going there is his antagonism towards Germany and German culture. Germany is riddled with all sorts of anti-Semitism. The Germans are resentful towards the Jews who are so successful. They fear the Jews will gain yet more power. Albert finds it hard to fathom why there's so strange a contrast between the Germans' hospitality and their hostility.

He also wants to be free of conventional nationalism. He wants Swiss citizenship.

He attempts to reassure Marie: 'If you were here at the moment, I would defy all reason and would give you a kiss for punishment and would have a good laugh at you, as you deserve, sweet little angel! And as to whether I will be patient? What other choice do I have with my beloved, naughty little angel?'

The tangled familial relationships produce unexpected outcomes during Albert's stay in Aarau. Maja is romantically attached to Marie's brother Paul. Anna Winteler becomes attached to Albert's new best friend, the engineer Michele Angelo Besso.

ANNA AND MICHELE

Six years older than Albert, Besso, born in Riesbach in Switzerland into a rambling family of Sephardic-Jewish-Italian descent, has an immediate appeal for Albert and vice versa. Albert first encounters him at a music evening at the house of Selina Caprotti. An ETH graduate with dark curly hair and nervous staring eyes, Besso has a philosophical passion for physics the equal of Albert's. He also shares a record of insubordination, having been expelled from high school for complaining about the inadequacies of his mathematics teacher.

He's enchanted by Besso who has just earned the displeasure of his superior; when asked to report on a power station, he misses the train, and on arrival finds he is unable to remember what he's supposed to do. When head office receives a card from Besso asking to be reminded, his superior says that Besso is 'completely useless and almost unbalanced'.

'Michele,' says Albert, 'is an awful *schlemiel*.'

He's Albert's kind of man, and Albert is devoted to him: 'Nobody else is so close to me, nobody knows me so well, nobody is so kindly disposed to me as you are.'

At one of Selina Caprotti's soirées, Albert introduces Besso to Anna Winteler and they fall in love.

The passage of light unseen, imagined is almost – as it were – visible.

Zürich instead of Berlin beckons.

Not before Albert and his friends embark upon a three-day June trek in the northeast of Switzerland along Säntis – at over 2,500 feet, the highest mountain in the Alpstein region. The ridge trail is precipitous. Albert is hopelessly ill-equipped to make the expedition. He ties his overcoat around him with his scarf. His shoes are cracked and split. Squinting into the drizzle, he leans heavily on his walking sticks.

The small group of classmates clamber uphill to Fälalp, an upper basin, then through patches of snow to an even steeper incline among loose rocks beneath a solitary needle of rock on the Rossmad peak. They head in a westerly direction to the bare, rocky ridge above the glacier. Albert gazes, captivated, at the nearby summits of the Churfirsten mountains to the west of Lake Zürich, to the east the mountain peaks of the Vorarlberg and to the north the Bodensee near Konstanz. The two-hour return hike to the Schwägalp is extremely steep in some places and requires considerable sure-footedness. He struggles to keep his balance on the razor edge and slips. He slides and rolls towards a sheer precipice.

He screams.

His nearest classmate, Adolf Frisch, stretches out his alpenstock.

Albert grabs hold of it for dear life and Frisch begins to pull him upwards to safety.

Frisch holds Albert in his arms. Albert is shaking, his face drenched in sweat.

'Put your head down between your knees,' Frisch tells him. 'Now sit still. Breathe slowly out. Breathe in.'

'Thanks, Adolf.'

'It's nothing.'

'Nothing? You saved my life.'

'Anyone would've done the same.'

'I'm sorry to be such a nuisance.'

'You're not a nuisance. To be honest you aren't cut out to be a mountaineer.'

In September 1896, aged seventeen, he passes the Swiss Matura with the highest grades in physics and mathematics. At last he can enrol at the polytechnic. Zürich becomes a reality.

The determination of his will and the intensity of his solitary mind studies will lead to him becoming arguably the greatest scientist who ever lived, with an intelligence that is far from normal.

ZÜRICH

There's a melancholic inevitability about the separation from Marie. She's accepted a teaching post in Olsberg, an isolated town in the Hochsauerland district of Westphalia, 570 kilometres distant.

Sensing one of life's new beginnings, the seventeen-year-old Albert disembarks at the Hauptbahnhof in Zürich with a spring in his step. He carries his battered violin case in one hand, his suitcase in the other, and walks out to the Bahnhofstrasse.

Beyond the River Limmat he can see the neoclassical buildings of the polytechnic and the University of Zürich. The mountains embrace old Zürich, its churches, hotels, restaurants and banks, and its Roman ruins and the lake, the Zürichsee, in the southeast. Trolley cars trundle and clank up the hills of the Zürichberg and the Uetliberg. Zürich prides itself on its Calvinistic heritage.

With a monthly allowance of 100 francs provided by Aunt Julie Koch, Albert can afford a room to rent in the student quarter with Frau Kägi at Unionstrasse 4, off Baschligplatz.

Albert relishes the intellectual and artistic ferment of *fin de siècle* Europe. Freud thinks of dreams and sexual hysteria in Vienna and publishes *The Interpretation of Dreams*. Stéphane Mallarmé experiments with silence and the random in a Paris dominated by the novelty of the Eiffel Tower. The Dreyfus Affair shakes France. On 13 January 1898, Émile Zola publishes an open letter in *L'Aurore* addressed to the president, Félix Faure, accusing the government of anti-Semitism and the unlawful jailing of Alfred Dreyfus, sentenced to penal servitude for life for espionage. Zola points out the judicial errors and the lack of evidence, and is himself prosecuted and found guilty of libel on 23 February 1898. He flees to England, returning to France the following year. The Paris Universal Exhibition of 1900 attracts 51 million visitors. In 1901, the first Nobel prizes are awarded. In the same year Kandinsky is a founding member of the art group Phalanx in Munich.

Stability and freedom is what Zürich offers. Jung, who comes to Zürich from Basel in 1900, finds the city 'relates to the world not by the intellect, but by commerce. Yet here the air was free and I had always valued that. Here you were not weighed down by the brown fog of the centuries, even though one missed the rich background of culture.' Rosa Luxemburg, Marxist and eventual founder of the Communist Party of Germany, and her cohorts were already living in the city among the students, free-thinkers and social outcasts. Thomas Mann publishes his first novel, *Buddenbrooks*, in 1901. Art nouveau is all the rage. In 1905 Henri Matisse exhibits *Le bonheur de vivre*. Two years later Picasso reinvents painting with *Les Demoiselles d'Avignon*.

The ETH (the Swiss Federal Institute of Technology), stands next to the university on Rämistrasse. Set back from the street is a small courtyard. Its open oak doors reveal arches, balconies, dimly lit by skylights and high windows.

Theoretical physics is just coming into its own as an academic discipline. Its pioneers, Max Planck in Berlin, Hendrik Lorentz in

Holland, and Ludwig Boltzmann in Vienna combine physics with mathematics to suggest territories that experimentalists have yet to explore. Mathematics is supposed to be a major part of Albert's compulsory studies at the polytechnic.

As for Marie, Albert has grown weary of their relationship.

When Albert gives a disingenuous hint that he plans to visit her in Aarau, Marie is thrilled. She vows that she will love him for eternity. Albert finds this cloying. She sends him a gift of a teapot.

He realises the one-sided relationship can't go on. He tells her bluntly that they should refrain from writing to each other.

Marie says she can't believe he really means this.

Albert finds it hard to disguise his irritation. The gift of a teapot goes down badly. He doesn't want a teapot.

She retaliates: 'The matter of my sending you the stupid little teapot does not have to please you at all as long as you are going to brew some good tea in it. Stop making that angry face which looked at me from all the sides and corners of the writing paper.'

He stops writing to her.

Marie writes to his mother for advice.

'The rascal has become frightfully lazy,' Pauline Einstein tells her. 'I have been waiting in vain for news for these last three days; I will have to give him a thorough talking-to once he's here.'

Albert tells Marie's mother that the relationship is over. He won't be coming to Aarau in springtime.

It would be more than unworthy of me to buy a few days of bliss at the cost of new pain, of which I have already caused too much to the dear child through my fault. It fills me with a peculiar kind of satisfaction that now I myself have to taste some of the pain that I brought upon the dear girl through my thoughtlessness and ignorance of her delicate nature. Strenuous intellectual work and looking at God's nature are the reconciling, fortifying yet relentlessly strict angels that shall lead me through all of life's troubles. If only I were able to give some of this to the good child. And yet, what a peculiar way this is to weather the storms of life – in many a lucid moment I appear to myself as an ostrich who buries his head in the desert sand so as not to perceive the danger.

Marie suffers an acute depression, whereas Albert's eyes focus on someone else.

HERE IS MILEVA

Five male students join the mathematics and physics class, and one woman, Mileva Maric, a twenty-year-old, slim Hungarian-Serb. Albert admires her seriousness. She seems almost as much of an outsider as he does. He notices the orthopaedic boots she wears. One leg is shorter than the other causing her to limp. He admires the lack of fuss with which she deals with her disability.

Mileva becomes friends with another student, Hélène Slavic from Vienna. Hélène is studying history. They have rooms with two Serb and two Croat women in a pension run by Fraulein Engelbrecht at Plattenstrasse 50, not far from Albert.

In one or other of the many cafés on Zürich's Baschligplatz, he holds forth to his friend Marcel Grossmann, from an old aristocratic Thalwil family.

Albert puffs at his long pipe: 'Listen to me. Atoms and mechanics are the concepts that will reduce natural phenomena to fundamental principles in the way geometry could be found in a few axioms or propositions.'

They rail against the pointless lives of the bourgeoisie, swearing never to be trapped by the petty and the provincial.

The friends consume vast amounts of coffee, bratwurst and tobacco; so much that they stain Albert's teeth brown. In the evenings he plays the violin for his friends. The Mozart Violin Sonata in E minor, and Sonata No. 6, K.301. Afterwards they use the telescope at the Eidgenössische Sternwarte, built by Gottfried Semper to look at the night sky. No sign of Mileva.

He pontificates in the physics labs in the hope that Mileva might be impressed. She stares at him and usually directs her stare sharply back to the task in hand. Work comes first. Albert recognises a fellow traveller. He glimpses her in the library and admires her wide and sensuous mouth. He catches sight of her with friends at a concert given by Theodor Billroth performing Brahms. Albert finds the very sight of her radiates powerful sensuality. Perhaps fearful of rejection, he is a passive suitor, waiting for her to make the first move, which she doesn't.

HEINRICH FRIEDRICH WEBER

At the same time Albert makes enemies. He bridles at the head of the physics department, Professor Heinrich Friedrich Weber, who's inordinately proud of the new building he's persuaded Siemens to build. Weber's predeliction is for the history of physics. Albert's passion is for the present and future of physics. Weber even makes no mention of Albert's hero, the mathematical physicist James Clerk Maxwell, whose pioneering equations accurately described the theory of electromagnetism.

Albert treats Weber with a cheeky informality, calling him 'Herr Weber', not 'Professor'. Weber forms a simmering dislike for Albert's cheek.

Albert is no slouch. Among other courses, he takes Weber's in Physics, Oscillations, Electromechanics, Theory of Alternating Current and Absolute Electrical Measurements.

Albert also studies alone. He's captivated by the series of brilliant experiments by Heinrich Hertz, who has discovered radio waves and established that James Clerk Maxwell's theory of electromagnetism is correct. Hertz has also discovered the photoelectric effect, providing one of the initial clues to the quantum world's existence.

Weber takes him to one side. 'You're a very clever boy, Einstein.'

'Thank you, Herr Weber.'

'Professor Weber. But you have one great fault. You'll never let yourself be told anything.'

Albert treats it as a compliment.

Then he causes offence to the other ETH professor, Jean Pernet, by playing truant from his course: Physical Experiments for Beginners. The small, plump Pernet demands Albert receive a *Verweis*: a strong official reprimand from the director.

Pernet calls Albert to his office. 'Your work has a measure of goodwill about it. You're eager enough. But you have a lack of capability. Why not give up physics. Study medicine, philology or law?'

Albert is silent.

'Well?' says Pernet.

'Because I feel I have a talent,' says Albert. 'Why can't I pursue physics?'

'Do what you want, Einstein. Do what you want. I am warning you. In your own interests.'

When Albert turns up at Pernet's next lecture he's given an instruction paper, which he ceremoniously dumps in the wastepaper basket.

Then he causes a sensation in Pernet's lab. A woman student struggles to seal a test tube with a cork. Pernet tells her the test tube will disintegrate.

'The man's insane,' Albert tells her. 'His rage made him faint the other day. Passed clean out in class.'

The test tube explodes. The blast damages Albert's right hand. He can't play the violin for several weeks.

47

Though he likes the mathematics professor, Hermann Minkowski, a thirty-year-old Russian Jew, he even plays truant from his lectures. Minkowski calls Albert 'a lazy dog'.

MARCEL GROSSMANN

His closest friend, Marcel Grossmann, is from an old Swiss family in Zürich. Albert admires Grossmann. He's a quick learner. The pair hang out at the Café Metropole by the River Limmat. Marcel tells his parents: 'One day this Einstein will be a great man.'

Music is a diversion from the inadequacies of the ETH. Bach. Schubert. Mozart. So is sailing alone on Lake Zürich.

Albert joins in the musical evenings at Fraulein Engelbrecht's pension at Plattenstrasse 50, where he turns up with his violin and physics books. Mileva plays the tamburitza and piano.

Albert also attends meetings of the Swiss branch of the Society for Ethical Culture.

He finds a political mentor, Gustav Maier, director of the

Brann department store, a popular figure on the scientific and cultural scene.

Now he summons up courage to issue an invitation to Mileva. He proposes she accompany him on a hiking expedition. *Eine Wanderung*. To look at the world from Zürich's Uetliberg mountain.

The day-trippers take the train from Zürich's Hauptbahnhof, riding up the Uezgi, entranced by the mountain blooms and blossoms.

'Look,' says Albert. '*Allium ursinum.*'

'What?'

'Wild garlic.'

At 2,850 feet, the Uetliberg towers over the rooftops of Zürich and the vivid blue lakes.

Albert puts his arm around her shoulders. 'There's the Reppisch Valley,' he tells her. 'Over there, the Bernese Alps, the Eiger, Mönch and Jungfrau.' He takes her hand. They gaze into each other's eyes.

He stoops down, picks a flower and holds it out to Mileva. 'For you.'

'For me?'

'For you.'

'What is it?'

'*Myosotis alpestris.* It's a forget-me-not. Promise me?'

'Anything.'

'Forget me not.'

She draws his mouth to hers. Her lips are full. Her tongue playful. He strokes her cheeks. Inhales her fragrance, cologne. He rubs his hand slowly up and down her back. She moans softly. They stand in silence, smiling.

On holiday in Milan his mother finds him transformed. The family laugh, play the piano and violin, and joke.

Albert immerses himself in the history of the Jewish community

49

of Milan, which is fairly recent, starting in the early nineteenth century. Before then, under the Sforza and Visconti, the Jews were permitted to stay for just a few days at a time in the city. Then, in the early 1800s, the restrictions were lifted. In 1892, the Central Synagogue was inaugurated.

He relishes the idea that Milan is also the only city in the world with a vineyard at its heart. He finds it in the courtyard of the House of Atellani on the Corso Magenta. Best of all, the owner of the vineyard had once been none other than Leonardo da Vinci. Albert is transported right back to 1490 when Leonardo planted it.

He plunges into reading da Vinci, sometimes writing out Leonardo's observations and thoughts that seem to confirm many of his own. He annotates Leonardo's remarks: *I know this to be true.*

When once you have tasted flight, you will forever walk the earth with your eyes turned skyward, for there you have been, and there you will always long to return. He who loves practice without theory is like the sailor who boards ship without a rudder and compass and never knows where he may cast.

Poor is the pupil that does not surpass his master.

The perspective of light is my perspective.

If the Lord – who is the light of all things – vouchsafe to enlighten me, I will treat of Light; wherefore I will divide the present work into 3 Parts . . . Linear Perspective, The Perspective of Colour, The Perspective of Disappearance.

Who will offer me a wage to exist? It vexes me greatly that having to earn my living has forced me to interrupt the work and to attend to small matters.

He thinks of Mileva. I love you. I love you, Mileva Maric.

'Gravitation is not responsible for people falling in love,' he mutters to himself.

Leonardo says: 'The act of procreation and anything that has any relation to it is so disgusting that human beings would soon die out if there were no pretty faces and sensuous dispositions.'

Ich liebe dich, Mileva. Ich liebe und verehre dich.

I love you, Mileva. I love and adore you.

He returns to Zürich in high spirits and makes straight for Plattenstrasse, only to be greeted by a thunderbolt. Mileva's landlady, Johanna Bachtöld, answers the door.

'Here to see Mileva?' she says.

'Yes.'

'She's left,' Fraulein Bachtöld says.

'She's what?'

'She's left. She's given up her studies.'

'Where's she gone?'

'Back to Hungary,' says Fraulein Bachtöld.

'How long for.'

'I don't know. For ever, I suppose.'

For four weeks Mileva keeps a baffling silence.

Albert assumes, rightly, that she must have gone home to Kac in Hungary, almost a thousand kilometres east of Zürich, to the family villa, the Spire, where Mileva was born.

As a bright, temperamental child, she does her best to disguise the hip dislocated at birth. She learns the piano and tries to dance.

Her father says her dancing reminds him of a wounded bird. The pattern of her education is as spidery as Albert's. Her father's postings as a civil servant mean that she attends Volksschule in Ruma; the Serbian Higher Girls' School in Novi Sad; the Kleine Real Schule in

51

Sremska Mitrovica, and other establishments in Sabac and Zagreb. She develops a passion for mathematics, which leads her to Zürich and to the ETH and Albert. And now? She's back home.

What drives her to go home is a mystery; perhaps even to herself. She doesn't communicate with Albert. Albert doesn't, or rather can't, communicate with her.

She once more begins travelling, west to Heidelberg, where she takes a room in the Hotel Ritter.

She introduces herself to Philipp Lenard, recently appointed professor of theoretical physics at the University of Heidelberg and a pioneer in the development of the cathode-ray tube, in which cathode rays produce a luminous image on a fluorescent screen.

Back in Zürich, after some nifty detective work among her friends, Albert discovers her whereabouts.

He writes to her asking her to get in touch. Her reply is long in coming. When it does Albert opens the envelope in a fever of excitement. His loved one writes:

I would have answered immediately to thank you for your sacrifice in writing, this repaying a bit of the enjoyment you had of me during our hike together – but you said I shouldn't write until I was bored – and I am very obedient (just ask Fraulein Bachtöld). I waited and waited for boredom to set in, but until today my waiting has been in vain, and I'm not sure what to do about it. On the one hand, I could wait until the end of time, but then you would think me a barbarian – on the other I still can't write to you with a clear conscience.

As you've already heard, I've been walking around under German oaks in the lovely Neckar valley, whose allure is unfortunately now bashfully cloaked in a thick fog. No matter how much I strain my eyes, that's all I see; it's as desolate and grey as infinity.

Papa gave me some tobacco that I'm to give you personally. He's eager to whet your appetite for our little land of outlaws. I told him all about you – you absolutely must come back with me someday – the two of you would really have a lot to talk about! But I'll have to play the role of interpreter. I can't send the tobacco, because should you have to pay duty on it, you would curse me *and* my present.

It really was too enjoyable in Prof. Lenard's lecture yesterday; now he's talking about the kinetic theory of gases. It seems that oxygen molecules travel at a speed of over 400m per second, and after calculating and calculating, the good professor set up equations, differentiated, integrated, substituted, and finally shows that the molecules in question actually do move at such a velocity, but that they only travel the distance of $\frac{1}{100}$ of a hair's breadth.

Best wishes, your Mileva

Mileva considers returning to Zürich.

The one misgiving her father has about her decision concerns the eighteen-year-old Albert. 'I know it amuses you that he has no interest in his clothes or grooming. That he's always losing his keys, leaves his suitcase on trains. You're four years older than he is. That's quite a gap.'

'Maybe,' she says. 'But he's my peer. He's someone I can talk to. He feels the same about me.'

'What are his job prospects?'

'He'll find work as a teacher somewhere, Papa. And his family has some money.'

'Do you love him, Mileva?'

'Yes, Papa. I do.'

'It shows, it shows.'

Albert writes to her as if she's a friend: 'Liebes Fräulein.' Then he playfully calls her '*Liebes Doxerl*', 'Dear Dollie'. She addresses him as *Johanzel*, Johnnie.

'Without you I lack self-confidence,' Albert writes, 'passion for work, and enjoyment of life, in short, without you, my life is no life. If only you could be here with me for a while! We understand one another's dark souls so well.'

Then comes news from Mileva that she has a goiter, an abnormal enlargement of her thyroid gland producing a large lump at the front of her neck.

The news appals Albert's parents. Mileva is obviously a disabled freak. Their insults mortify him.

Mileva spends her time on solitary walks along the river banks and in the forests. She is highly amused by the copy of Mark Twain's *A Tramp Abroad* that Albert sends her. He underlines:

In German, a young lady has no sex, while a turnip has. Think what overwrought reverence that shows for the turnip, and what callous disrespect for the girl. See how it looks in print – I translate this from a conversation in one of the best of the German Sunday-school books:

Gretchen: 'Wilhelm, where is the turnip?'
Wilhelm: 'She has gone to the kitchen.'
Gretchen: 'Where is the accomplished and beautiful English maiden?'
Wilhelm: 'It has gone to the opera.'

Alone, she attends lectures, reads in the library or visits the Kurpfälzisches Museum of art and archaeology in the Palais Morass.

Her solitude proves too much, the distance from Albert too far. She pines for him. So she goes back to Zürich.

For their final ETH dissertations, Albert and Mileva both elect to write on heat conduction. Albert is awarded 4.5 out of 6; Mileva 4. He is successful in the final examination, coming fourth out of five. Mileva fails and plans to retake the examination in twelve months. The polytechnic's qualification enables him to teach mathematics and science in secondary school – if he wants to: and he doesn't. Albert sets his sights on a job. Weber blocks him and their relationship collapses. Albert's relations with his mother grow fraught. Pauline writes, 'You ought to have a wife. By the time you're thirty she'll be an old witch. If she gets pregnant you'll really be in a mess.' Albert replies that they haven't 'been living in sin'.

Funds run short. They support themselves by offering private tuition. Albert applies for posts in Leiden, Vienna and Berlin. Most of his letters remain unanswered.

Albert is convinced it's Weber who's blocking his progress.

'There's no point writing any more letters to professors,' he tells Mileva.

'You must.'

'Weber will only give them yet another bad recommendation. I will soon have graced all the physicists from the North Sea to the southern tip of Italy with my offers to work in their departments.'

Mileva becomes withdrawn, her moodiness and depression noticed with concern by their friends, above all by Albert. He compliments her on her clothes, her hair. He plays Mozart for her. To no avail. She is obsessed with her work, with scientific truth.

He suggests a change of scenery. He proposes he take her on an idyllic secret holiday.

'I am not sure,' she says, gazing at him with solemnity. 'I have work to do. So do you. And Como – all those women with lady's maids stuffed into suffocating bone corsets.'

'We don't need to have anything to do with them. You will like the cuisine.'

'How do you know?'

'You told me you like fish.'

'Did I?'

'You said you like perch.'

Mileva smiles.

'There's a traditional dish we'll have. *Risotto al Pesce Persico*, prepared with white wine, onion, butter and rice. We can dine in style against the backdrop of snow-capped peaks.'

'You're determined to take me?'

'Yes.'

'Very well.'

COMO
***

On Sunday 5 May 1901, early in the morning, he waits for her at Stazione di Como San Giovanni in a fever of anticipation.

At the side of Lake Bellagio, Albert asks her: 'What's your favourite book?'

'*First Serbian Mathematics* by Vasilije Damjanović.'

'Your hero?'

'Alexander the Great.'

'Alexander the Great?'

'Because he loved scientific research and medicine.'

'What's your favourite place?' asks Mileva.

'The Milky Way. The heavenly space. My space.'

This is where he can free himself from fear.

They explore the Duomo di Como, Italy's last Gothic cathedral. They stroll arm-in-arm in wonder through the gardens of Villa Carlotta, among the rhododendrons, azaleas and tropical plants; cedars, sequoias and huge plane trees.

They embrace in front of Tadolini's copy of Canova's *Eros and Psyche*, then spend the night together in a small hotel and next day hire a sleigh, travelling wrapped in coats and shawls into the mountains.

Albert takes up an appointment in Schaffhausen in northern Switzerland, working as a private tutor.

Mileva lives on her own in Stein am Rhein, some nineteen kilometres distant. Albert visits her there once a week. He finds her suffering from the emotional strains generated by their separations and the opposition from his family to their relationship. His mother obstinately declares she will have nothing to do with Mileva.

Albert joins Mileva on a rainy summer day in a café overlooking the Rhine. He finds her unusually happy and is full of compliments.

'You look so happy and well.'

'I am.'

'I'm so lucky to have found you, a creature who's my equal in every way.'

She reaches out for his hand. 'Albert. Feel my stomach. There are going to be three of us.'

Albert sits bolt upright, beaming. The words stick in his throat.

Then he staggers to his feet, embraces Mileva and weeps. 'Our child will be a girl.'

'You don't know.'

'I know. We'll call her Lieserl. We'll keep her a secret.'

'That's what I want too. I'll have the child at home in Novi Sad.'

They hold hands and smile through tears of joy.

Once he gains Swiss citizenship, Albert finds a job as a substitute teacher at a Winterthur high school, the Technikum Winterthur, sixteen kilometres from the city centre. His duties take up six hours in the mornings. The rest of the time he works at home. Soon afterwards he changes tack, answering an advertisement in a teachers' journal to prepare a student at Jakob Nüesch Realschule at Schaffhausen. By now he has to face up to the fact that no one will give him a job.

'Who knows,' he says, 'I may have to play my violin in the streets and beg for a living.'

BERN

In 1902, Michael Grossmann brings good news. He persuades Albert, now twenty-three, to take up a job at the Swiss National Patent Office in Bern as a technical expert, Class 3. The annual salary is a satisfactory 3,500 francs. Albert is to work six days a week, from 8 a.m. to 4 p.m., in Bern's Postal and Telegraph Building.

'There's no doubt any more,' Albert writes to Mileva. 'Soon you'll be my happy little wife, just watch. Now our troubles are over. Only now this terrible weight is off my shoulders do I realise how much I truly love you. Soon I'll be able to take my Dollie in my arms and call her my own in front of the whole world. We'll work on science together, so we don't become old philistines.'

No sooner has he found rooms than he receives bad news from Milan. His father's health is deteriorating.

Albert finds the fifty-five-year-old Hermann terminally ill with a heart condition.

Albert asks his father to give his consent to his marrying Mileva. He is far from confident Hermann will agree to give it. Aside from anything else, it will be the first time any Einstein has married a gentile. Hermann though does give his consent, just three days before his death. He asks his family to leave the room so he can die alone.

Albert feels a terrible guilt that he isn't with his father when he dies.

Milos Maric, Mileva's father – Serbian army officer, judge – views his daughter's condition as unwelcome, to say the least. The child could be farmed out to relatives, it could be adopted. Turn-of-the-century Switzerland has no place for illegitimacy. Albert realises, as indeed does Mileva, that the cards are stacked against them. At the ETH he has a reputation for arrogance, ill manners and lack of respect. He has alienated the supporters he needs. Mileva is Slav. He is a Jew. To add an illegitimate child to the mix might prove the last straw in so far as his prospects are concerned. With both families against them, Albert and Mileva are thrown together in isolation.

Bern itself offers Albert some consolation. The Aare River circles the city. It's still largely a fifteenth-century city of arcades, cobblestone streets and fountains. Albert calls it 'an ancient, exquisitely cozy city, in which one lives exactly as in Zürich'.

He finds a room on Gerechtigkeitsgasse in the old part of the city: Justice Alley, together with Kramgasse in the city centre, is watched over by Hans Gieng's fountain figure, Lady Justice, on the Gerechtigkeitsbrunnen. The blindfolded statue dwarfs Albert, who's 5 feet 7½ inches.

She's holding the sword of justice in her right hand.

'D'you like the statue?' Mileva asks.

'So long as she loves Justice as much as we love each other.'

Mileva's father sends Albert the news: Mileva has given birth to a baby girl, Lieserl.

'Is she healthy?' Albert writes to Milos. 'What are her eyes like? Which of us does she more resemble? Who is giving her milk? Is she hungry? She must be completely bald. I love her so much and don't even know her yet!'

But Albert remains in Bern. He tells no one about Lieserl, the child he says he loves so much.

Mileva declares cryptically to Albert, 'I don't think we should say anything about Lieserl yet.'

He has other projects, so does not object.

SOLOVINE, HABICHT AND ALBERT

With Maurice Solovine, a philosophy student, and Conrad Habicht, son of a banker, Albert discusses philosophy of science. They call themselves the Olympia Academy.

Together they read Cervantes' *Don Quixote*, Sophocles' *Antigone*, Hume's *A Treatise of Human Nature*, Ernst Mach's *The Science of Mechanics* and *Analysis of the Sensations*, Spinoza's *Ethics* and Poincaré's *Science and Hypothesis*. These were the sources of Albert's own philosophy of science.

The three become the closest friends. When Solovine misses a planned meeting in his flat, having decided to go to a concert instead, he leaves a meal for Albert and Habicht with a note: 'Beloved friends, hard-boiled eggs and greetings.' Afterwards, Albert and Habicht re-arrange the rooms, moving furniture, books, plates, cups, knives and forks and spoons. Tobacco smoke fills the place. They leave a message: 'Dearest friend, thick smoke and greetings.' All three find it very amusing.

*

Solovine and Habicht speculate about Mileva's child. It's not difficult for them to have put two and two together. You only have to use your eyes: she's obviously given birth. But why hasn't Albert been to Serbia to see the child? Perhaps it's been put out for adoption? Perhaps it has succumbed to the scarlet-fever epidemic? If the latter, then it's most probable Albert or Mileva would've said something.

Neither Solovine nor Habicht think it proper to question Albert or Mileva on the subject. After all, what could either of them do to get an answer?

They recall Pythagoras: 'It is better either to be silent, or to say things of more value than silence.'

And decide not to raise the subject.

More than six years after they first met, and twelve months after the birth of Lieserl, on Tuesday 6 January 1903, Solovine and Habicht call a special session of the Olympia Academy so the pair can witness Albert's marriage to Mileva at Bern's register office. Pauline is absent. Albert is the first Einstein to take a non-Jewish wife. The ceremony is brief.

Albert, Mileva, Solovine and Habicht spend the rest of the day in bars and cafés drinking wine, eating sausages, Gruyére and ice cream. Albert plays his violin.

Herr and Frau Einstein return to their attic apartment on tranquil Tillierstrasse 18 on the right bank of the Aare, only to find Albert's lost the key and they have to disturb another resident to get in.

Next month they both fall victim to the influenza epidemic that has Switzerland in its grip. In Bern, 18,000 have succumbed.

Albert confides to Besso, 'Now I am a married man and am living a very pleasant, cozy life with my wife. She takes excellent care of everything, cooks well, and is always cheerful.'

Mileva writes to a friend: 'I am, if possible, even more attached to my dear treasure than I already was in the Zürich days. He is my only companion and society and I am happiest when he is beside me.'

Albert tries to accept the routines of the bourgeois life but fails.

At the suggestion of Dr Josef Sauter, a patent-office colleague, he takes refuge in Bern's Natural History Society, which meets in the Hotel Storchen at Spitalgasse 21. Albert enjoys the company, its talks and discussions. In the society's minutes of 2 May, the secretary records: 'The membership of Mr Alb. Einstein, mathematician at the patent office, is approved.'

On 5 December 1903 Albert gives his first lecture to the society on the theory of electromagnetic waves.

MILEVA, ALBERT AND HANS ALBERT, 1904

After a difficult pregnancy, Mileva gives birth to their first son, Hans Albert, on 14 May 1904, at Kramgasse 49. Albert and Mileva dote on the child. Albert shares his son's laughter and plays with him at bath-time. Mileva adapts to the domestic routine.

Albert becomes a popular and valued member of the patent-office staff. His position is established as permanent and he forms a close friendship with Michele Besso. They enjoy their shared satisfaction that people who understand physics know that the distinction between past, present and future is an illusion. Albert's energy and confidence are renewed.

For Mileva, it's the opposite. She's increasingly moody and jealous of his work. The stench of nappies and smoke from the fire fills the apartment – cold in winter, hot and foul-smelling in summer. Albert builds toy vehicles for Albertli with matchboxes and string. He regales the child with stories and plays lullabies for him on his violin. He holds Albertli with one hand on his knee and writes with the other. She is no more Albert's close scientific associate. Her job is chiefly that of cook and nursemaid. She's scared by her loneliness, the lack of companion-ship, the isolation. She craves someone to chat to.

She sits by the upstairs window watching the comings and goings on Kramgasse and the happy customers of the restaurant Zum untern Junker below. Time passes slowly, marked by the chimes from the clock tower 200 metres distant.

►►►►► THREE ►►►►►

1905

Annus Mirabilis

With a look of mischief in his watery eyes, Albert told me that when he and Mileva moved into their cramped third-floor apartment at 49 Kramgasse, in the old city centre of Bern, he couldn't really have predicted that 1905 would be the most extraordinary year of his life. Neither could his obscure civil servant friends.

Mimi Beaufort, Princeton, 1955

In the quiet of the patent office in Bern, Albert, aged twenty-six, perches on his stool, his mass of hair framing his large head. His shabby tweed jacket and trousers are too short. He wears no socks. The cloud of smoke from his cheap Villiger cigar hangs in the air. He occupies his time with reviews and papers for the most prestigious of German physics journals, *Annalen der Physik*.

In March 1905 he establishes the idea that light consists of minute particles which he calls 'photons', and that the universe is made out of distinct chunks of matter and energy.

Next month and in May he publishes two papers in *Annalen der Physik.*

The movement of atoms and molecules gives rise to heated scientific debate. Professor Ernst Mach and Professor Wilhelm Ostwald are among those who disparage Albert's ideas. Ostwald in particular advocates the view that thermodynamics deals only with energy and how it is transformed in the everyday world. Along with Mach, he argues that the laws of thermodynamics need not be based on mechanics, which dictate the existence of invisible atoms in motion.

Albert won't let any of this get in his way. Next he describes a new method for counting and determining the size of atoms or molecules in a given space. In the next paper he applies the molecular theory of heat to liquids to explain the so-called puzzle of Brownian motion. In 1827, the Scottish botanist Robert Brown suspended pollen in water, and observed that the pollen moved about irregularly in swarms.

Albert argues that if tiny yet visible particles are suspended in a liquid, the invisible atoms in the liquid bombard the suspended particles and make them jiggle about. He explains the motion in great detail and predicts the irregular, random motions of the particles under a microscope.

In May, he writes to Conrad Habicht, who's taken a post as a mathematics and physics teacher at the Protestant Educational Institute in Schiers in Switzerland. He promises to send Habicht four revolutionary papers.

The first deals with radiation and the energy properties of light and is very revolutionary . . . The second paper is a determination of the true size of atoms . . . The third proves that bodies of the order of magnitude $\frac{1}{1000}$mm, suspended in liquids, must already perform an observable random motion that is produced by thermal motion. Such movement . . . has actually been observed by physiologists who call it Brownian molecular motion. The fourth paper is only a rough draft at this point, and is an electrodynamics of moving bodies which employs a modification of the theory of space and time.

It is the 'very revolutionary' June paper which offers a guide to his arguments. What does the universe consists of: atoms, electrons? Space and time are mysterious; indeed, intangible.

'According to the assumption to be considered here, when a light ray is propagated from a point, the energy is not continuously distributed over an increasing space but consists of a finite number of energy quanta which are localised at points in space and which can be produced and absorbed only as complete units.'

He hardly expects people to follow his arguments.

'I want to know how God creates this world . . . the rest are details. What I'm really interested in is whether God could have made the world in a different way; that is, whether the necessity of logical simplicity leaves any freedom at all.'

His work is frenzied. He now applies relativity to produce his equation between mass and energy: m and E. Simply put, he finds that when an object approaches the speed of light – c – the mass of the object increases. As the object travels faster so it becomes heavier. Suppose it moved at the speed of light (which is impossible), then its mass and energy would be infinite.

Finally, his fifth paper, his doctoral dissertation, is entitled 'A New Determination of Molecular Dimensions'.

With $E = mc^2$ Albert is the first to propose that the equivalence of mass and energy is a general principle and a result of the symmetries of space and time.

Mileva is not alone in asking: 'What happens if your theory of relativity is refuted?'

'In that case I'd have to feel sorry for God, because the theory is correct.'

Albert, Mileva and Hans Albert move to a larger apartment in Bern: Besenscheuerweg 28, not far from the Gurten mountain.

For over a month Albert works in a frenzy at the patent office and at home by the light of an oil lamp. He has no time to record the progress of his thinking other than, of course, the evidence of his research.

Vastly enjoying the pursuit of the nature of matter, energy, motion, time and space, he seems to be unaware of the hour of the day, the day of the week or the date of the month. 'When I am doing something with complete enjoyment I don't notice that the time passes.'

'Is that why you're always late home?' Mileva asks.

'Not always.'

'Always.'

He decides to submit his dissertation for a PhD to Alfred Kleiner, professor of experimental physics at the University of Zürich. Kleiner is impressed: 'The arguments and calculations to be carried out are among the most difficult in hydrodynamics.' So too is the professor of mathematics, Heinrich Burkhardt: 'The mode of treatment demonstrates fundamental mastery of the relevant mathematical methods. What I checked, I found to be correct without exception.' Kleiner however says the dissertation is too short. Albert adds a single sentence, resubmits, and his dissertation is accepted. Albert can now call himself Dr Einstein.

That summer, Dr and Frau Einstein, with Hans Albert in tow, travel to Novi Sad.

Albert visits the Matica srpska, the oldest Serbian literary, cultural and scientific institution, founded in Pest in 1826 and which moved to Novi Sad in 1864. The library of the Matica Srpska contains approximately 3 million publications and its art gallery is the largest and most respected in Novi Sad. Albert is captivated.

Mileva's family, to Albert's surprise and delight, is warmly welcoming. They are moved that Albert treats her as his intellectual equal.

Albert carries his laughing son through the streets on his shoulders as if he's won a trophy. He deals with his anxieties about the fate of his lost child, Lieserl, by burying them. Did she die of scarlet fever, her corpse incinerated as another victim of this plague? Or is she alive, the victim of some tragic disability? Albert stays silent. The mystery of the girl's fate remains.

On his return to Bern, Albert is promoted to technical expert, Class 2, at the patent office. His salary is upped to 4,500 francs a year. So they move again, this time to a wood-framed house on Aegertenstrasse, a tree-lined street overlooking the River Aare.

He writes to Solovine, who's in Paris and whom he much misses, 'I am a federal ink-pisser, play the violin and ride my physical mathematical hobbyhorse.'

On Sundays Albert and Mileva arrange informal gatherings at home attended by Michele Besso, his wife Anna, and Maja, now in Bern working on her PhD.

Albert still entertains dreams of the years in Aarau while at the same time being tortured by a sense of guilt about Marie, who showed him so much kindness while he caused her only sorrow and pain.

His longings and reveries for his lovers and teachers now distant excite him more than Mileva, who presently shows him love and affection, but who he keeps at arm's length. Demonstrations of love are not to his taste. They trap him as much as, even more than, the bourgeois routines he despises. Lurking somewhere in his psyche is the fear of madness.

This is exacerbated by the news that Paul Winterer's brother Julius has returned from America and, mentally deranged, shot and killed his mother and brother-in-law, then shot himself.

Albert thinks of Michele Besso, whose brother, Marco, had taken his own life aged eighteen.

Albert's view is: 'If you want to live a happy life, tie it to a goal, not to people or things.'

That doesn't help him handle the latest news about Marie. Acute depression and mental irregularities have overtaken her as a result of their break-up. The doctors confine her to the Waldau Clinic in Bern.

DR GOTTLIEB BURCKHARDT

Albert enquires about the clinic and discovers that one Dr Gottlieb Burckhardt is conducting experimental surgery at Waldau: lobotomy, a psychosurgical procedure to solve the effects of schizophrenia. Burckhardt has performed lobotomies on half a dozen patients, with a 50 per cent success rate. Albert prays that Burckhardt won't get his hands on Marie.

He retreats into his work, writing more papers and reviews. Back home he plays games with Albertli obsessively: a spinning top and dancing teddy bears.

The games enrapture Albert as much as they do Albertli. Father and son rejoice in magic lantern shows. Albert buys a Gloria projector made by Ernst Planck of Nuremberg and becomes a skilled projectionist; to Albertli's delight, by moving the slides quickly, the images on the screen appear to move.

ALFRED KLEINER

It falls to Alfred Kleiner, professor of experimental physics at the University of Zürich, to make the official recommendation for Albert to be enlisted at the university.

Kleiner has no doubt about Albert's abilities. 'Einstein ranks among the most important theoretical physicist and has been recognised as such since his work on the relativity principle.'

Kleiner senses the anti-Semites will block Albert's appointment. The faculty committee records that:

The expression of our colleague Kleiner, based on several years of personal contact, were all the more valuable for the committee as well as for the faculty as a whole since Herr Dr Einstein is an Israelite and since precisely to the Israelites among scholars are inscribed (in numerous cases not entirely without cause) all kinds of unpleasant peculiarities of character such as intrusiveness, impudence and a shopkeeper's mentality in the perception of their academic position. It should be said, however, that also among the Israelites there exist men who do not exhibit a trace of these disagreeable qualities and it is not proper, therefore, to disqualify a man only because he happens to be a Jew. Indeed, one occasionally finds people also among non-Jewish scholars who in regard to a commercial perception and utilisation of their academic profession develop qualities that are usually considered as specifically Jewish. Therefore, neither the committee nor the faculty as a whole considered it compatible with its dignity to adopt anti-Semitism as a matter of policy.

Albert wonders what the committee has said. He learns it voted ten in support of him, with one abstention.

He senses the current of anti-Semitism beneath the surface of academic and social life. When he hears the university salary offered is less than he's paid at the patent office, he declines the offer.

Zürich comes back with an increased offer. This time he accepts. 'So,' he tells his correspondent the Polish physicist Jakob Laub, 'now I am an official member of the guild of whores.'

* * *

In Zürich, the family budget is stretched to the limit. So Mileva takes in lodgers.

The main thing is that Albert has now entered the academic world. Stability is on the cards.

His fame is spreading. Who could've guessed that the immediate future would be so different – that during the next five years Albert will shift between three universities in as many countries, and the ETH?

'I cannot tell you', Mileva writes to a friend, 'how happy we are because of this change which will free Albert of his daily eight hours in the office, and he will now be able to devote himself to his beloved science, and *only* science.' Moreover, Mileva continues: 'He is now regarded as the best of the German-language physicists, and they give him a lot of honours. I am very happy for his success, because he really does deserve it; I only hope and wish that fame does not have a harmful effect on his humanity.'

His correspondence increases. Fellow physicists throughout Europe seek him out.

His lectures are popular. Humorous, informal and quixotic, he speaks without notes. He invites his small audiences to interrupt him if they don't understand a point. He even interrupts himself.

He likes being a Swiss citizen. He likes Switzerland. All he requires is peace to think. A pencil and paper. Some sailing on a nearby lake. His life turns like Albertli's spinning top.

The Naturforschende Gesellschaft in Zürich, the Society for Natural Sciences, elects him a member. In addition to physics it devotes itself to natural history and mathematics.

Then he receives the offer of a post at the German University in Prague. The chair of theoretical physics has fallen vacant. This will mean he is a full professor with the appropriate salary.

And for the third time Mileva falls pregnant.

Eduard Einstein is born on 28 July 1910. It's a difficult birth. Mileva is weak and unwell. Her doctor tells Albert to find money to pay a servant. A slanging match ensues during which Mileva takes Albert's side: 'Can't you see that my husband works himself to the bone.'

'You need help,' the doctor tells her.

A compromise is reached. Mileva's mother is called upon and arrives from Novi Sad to busy herself around the house.

Mileva's moods grow darker.

She confides in Albert: 'You see, I long for love, and I would so rejoice if I could hear an affirmative reply that I almost believe it is the fault of the damned science, so I gladly accept your smile on that account.'

She is acutely aware of her losses. Her career as a physicist is over, Lieserl is gone. Was the child given up for adoption? Her whereabouts, alive or dead, are unknown. Outwardly and inwardly, Albert refuses to address the subject. Her fate is a nightmare he will not face. Fortunately, little Albertli is full of fun. And at least now there's 'Tete'.

Albert writes to his mother in Berlin: 'To dwell on the things that depress or anger us does not help in overcoming them. One must knock them down alone. It is most probable that I will be offered the position of full professor at a large university with a significantly better salary than I have now.'

He has developed an appetite for continual travelling. To satisfy it he decides to visit two of his heroes, Hendrik Lorentz and Ernst Mach. Lorentz shared the 1902 Nobel Prize with his fellow Dutchman Pieter Zeeman for the discovery of the Zeeman effect: 'in recognition of the extraordinary service they rendered by their researches into the influence of magnetism upon radiation phenomena'. Ernst Mach was the first physicist to study supersonic motion, and his critique and rejection of Newton's notion regarding time and space is one inspiration for Albert's theory of relativity.

He visits Mach in Vienna in 1911. Mach is by now a virtual

recluse in his seventies, partially paralysed and almost stone deaf. 'Let us suppose', Albert shouts, 'that by assuming the existence of atoms in a gas we were able to predict an observable property of this gas that could not be predicted on the basis of non-atomic theory, would you then accept such a hypothesis?'

'This hypothesis might be an economical one.'

Which Albert takes as acceptance.

WITH HENDRIK LORENTZ

Albert has long profoundly admired Hendrik Lorentz. Theoretical physicists the world over regard the Dutch free-thinker as the leading spirit of physics. It's Lorentz who prepares the way for the positive reception of quantum theory. Albert has used many of Lorentz's mathematical tools, concepts and results to produce the theory of special relativity. 'I admire this man like no other,' he tells Laub. 'I might say – I love him.' Albert and Mileva visit Lorentz in Leiden, where they stay with him and his wife, Aletta.

Lorentz beguiles Albert with his charm and hospitality, becoming a father-figure; lucid, generous, ready to advise Albert, to correct the smallest detail. Albert considers Lorentz's mind to be as 'beautiful as a good work of art'.

His mind is whirling with the various opportunities facing him. He decides to take up the post at the Charles-Ferdinand University in Prague, only to find that the Zürich faculty is keen to keep him. A petition is launched: 'Professor Einstein has an amazing talent for presenting the most difficult problems of theoretical physics so clearly and so comprehensively that it is a great delight for us to follow his lectures, and he is so good at establishing a perfect rapport with his audience.'

He's offered a salary increase of 1,000 francs, a tempting offer, resisted, and the family moves to Prague.

Pozdrav z Prahy!

PRAGUE

They occupy a new flat in Smichov, Trebížského 1215, on the left bank of the Moldau. His walk to work takes twenty minutes.

'I have here a splendid institute in which I work comfortably,' he writes to Besso . . . Only the people are so alien to me.' He hates the Teutonic bureaucrats. The staff bow and scrape. His office has a view of the Royal County Insane Asylum. He tells visitors: 'Those are the madmen who do not occupy themselves with the quantum theory.' Isolated, he writes papers.

The flat in Smichov has electricity; a live-in maid is a bonus.

He becomes a regular at the Café Louvre, an art nouveau café on Národní trída, and meets Max Brod and Kafka, or goes to Berta Fanta's salon on Old Town Square, where he plays the violin for the intellectual elite, including the philosophers Rudolf Steiner and Hugo Bergmann.

Albert readily makes new friendships with such like-minded thinkers and scientists. One of these is a young Jewish physicist from Vienna, Paul Ehrenfest. Albert and Mileva take to entertaining him at their house.

PAUL EHRENFEST WITH ALBERT AND HANS ALBERT

Ehrenfest accompanies Albert's playing of Brahms on the violin, and Hans Albert sings along.

Ehrenfest describes something of his background. 'My father, Sigmund, slaved in a wool mill in Loschwitz in Moravia. After he married my mama they moved to Vienna and set up as grocers. The locals were anti-Semites. I'm the youngest of five boys. I was sickly.'

'I often wonder,' says Albert, 'whether or not it is the lot of scientists to have had sickly childhoods.'

'It is the other way round,' says Mileva. 'Sickly children are more likely to be scientists.'

'It is an interesting conundrum,' says Albert. 'How old were you, Paul, when you learned to read and write and count?'

'Six.'

'I was younger.'

'Don't boast,' says Mileva.

'My mother died of breast cancer twenty years ago,' says Ehrenfest. 'Is yours still alive?'

'Yes. Forty-eight. In Württemberg.'

'She's fifty, Albert.'

'Is she? Fifty. I rely upon you, dearest, to do the mathematics . . . what's happened to your father?'

'He's married to a woman the same age as my eldest brother.'

'And you, at school?'

'I was useless. I managed to get a place at the Technische Hochschule in Vienna in October 1899, and attended Boltzmann's lectures on the mechanical theory of heat during 1899 and 1900. Two years later I moved to Göttingen where I saw this young Russian mathematics student, Tatyana Alexeyevna Afanasyeva from Kiev. Why didn't she come to meetings of the mathematics club?'

'Because she wasn't allowed to,' says Mileva.

'Right. So I protested. Got the rules changed. And married Tatyana. $E = mc^2$.'

Albert laughs.

'I stayed put in Vienna without a post. I returned to Göttingen in September 1906, hoping there might be a position available but there wasn't. And I learned – it was terrible – Boltzmann had committed suicide on 6 September. I wrote his obituary. He hanged himself.'

'What really happened?' Albert asks.

'He was holidaying with his wife and youngest daughter, Elsa, at the Hotel Ples in the Italian village of Duino near Trieste on the Adriatic. He was scheduled to return to Vienna on the following day for a new series of lectures on theoretical physics. He dreaded giving them. Frau Boltzmann and Elsa were swimming. Back at the hotel he found a window cord and hanged himself in his room. Elsa found her father's body. It seems he'd been suffering from neurasthenia. But . . . suicide. Elsa can't speak a word about it.'

Tears roll down Albert's cheeks.

Mileva seeks to change the subject. 'You went to St Petersburg?'

'In 1907,' Ehrenfest says. 'I had mixed feelings about the anti-Semitism. Tatyana and I collaborated on an article about statistical mechanics. It took us a long time. I toured universities in the German-speaking world in the hope of a position.'

'So did I,' says Albert.

'Saw Planck in Berlin, Herglotz in Leipzig, Sommerfeld in Munich. To Zürich. To Vienna, where I heard that Poincaré had written a paper on quantum theory that gave similar results to mine in the *Annalen der Physik* paper. Then Sommerfeld recommended me to Lorentz to take up his chair in Leiden.'

Ehrenfest produces a piece of paper and hands it to Albert.

Albert reads aloud: '"He lectures like a master. I have hardly ever heard a man speak with such fascination and brilliance. Significant phrases, witty points and dialectic are all at his disposal in an extra-ordinary manner . . . He knows how to make the most difficult things concrete and intuitively clear. He translates mathematical arguments into easily comprehensible pictures."'

'Could have been talking about me,' says Albert.

Mileva gets to her feet with difficulty. 'Don't just talk about yourself, Albert.'

Mileva leaves the two men alone and Albert talks at length to Ehrenfest about his struggle to generalise his relativity theory. Ehrenfest proves to be a perfect sounding board.

After Ehrenfest's departure, Albert's thoughts and ambitions turn towards Berlin. He struggles with his misgivings about the place. The future of physics seems to depend on Berlin. He turns his mind to a more immediate engagement: the first Solvay Conference in Brussels.

THE FIRST SOLVAY CONFERENCE

Held between 30 October and 3 November 1911 under the patronage of the industrialist Ernest Solvay, this is the first international conference in the history of science. It brings together Europe's leading physicists for discussions on radiation and the quanta. Each is paid 1,000 francs to attend. Albert is immensely proud to have been invited. The scientists travel by train in heavily upholstered luxury to Brussels from Berlin, Leiden, Göttingen, Zürich, Paris, Vienna.

The Solvay Conference marks Albert's debut on the stage of international science. Chaired by Hendrik Lorentz, speaking Dutch, German and French, the delegates gather together to consider the two approaches to the subject: classical physics and quantum theory. Albert, at thirty-two years old, is the second youngest physicist present; Frederick Lindemann, at twenty-five, the youngest. Others include Marie Slodowska-Curie and Henri Poincaré.

These luminaries don't intimidate Albert. He laughingly refers to the conference as 'the Witches' Sabbath in Brussels'. The other physicists recognise him as the new star of their profession. Madame Curie praises Albert's clarity of mind, the enormity of his documentation, and his depth of knowledge. Poincaré declares that Albert is 'one of the most original thinkers I have ever met. What one has to admire in him above all is the facility with which he adapts himself to new concepts and knows how to draw from them every possible conclusion.' Frederick Lindemann and Louis de Broglie share the view that 'of all those present, Einstein and Poincaré moved in a class by themselves'.

After the formal proceedings, debate centres on relativity. Albert finds that Poincaré doesn't get it. The French, on the other hand, do.

Of all the delegates, he finds the trio of younger French physicists the most sympathetic, Paul Langevin, Jean Perrin and Marie Skłodowska-Curie.

He writes to Besso: 'I have not made any further progress in electron theory.' He tells Besso that the congress has 'an aspect similar to the wailing at the ruins of Jerusalem'. Nothing positive comes out of it. 'My treatment of fluctuations aroused great interest, but elicited no serious objection. I did not benefit much, as I did not hear anything which was not known to me already.'

Yet, in his bread-and-butter letter to Ernest Solvay, Albert writes: 'I thank you sincerely for the extremely beautiful week, which you provided us in Brussels, and not the least for your hospitality. The Solvay Congress shall always remain one of the most beautiful memories of my life.'

And not only because of the formal and informal discussions about physics but because he is both taken aback and intrigued by the scandal that two of his new French friends create.

Maria Skłodowska had met Pierre Curie in Paris in 1894 and they married a year later, Maria adopting the French spelling of her name.

MARIE CURIE

PAUL LANGEVIN

The Curies worked together on radioactivity, elaborating on the work of Röntgen and Henri Becquerel. In July 1898, they announced the discovery of polonium, a new chemical element, and on 20 December they announced the discovery of another, radium, the radioactive element crucial to the development of X-rays and radiology.

Together, along with Becquerel, they were awarded the Nobel Prize in Physics in 1903. Marie is the first woman to have a Nobel Prize.

Three years later, a horse-drawn carriage hits Pierre near the Pont Neuf and kills him. Marie is left with two daughters, aged nine and two. She takes over his teaching post, the first woman to teach at the Sorbonne, and applies herself to the work that they had begun together. She receives a second Nobel Prize, for Chemistry, in 1911, the announcement coinciding with the Solvay Conference. Albert is well aware that Marie is a controversial figure in France who receives the unwelcome attentions of the French press. When it is proposed she be elevated to the Académie des Sciences, the journalists launch attacks on her fuelled by anti-Semitism, misogyny, xenophobia and opposition to science and scientists in general. The worst of the attacks appear in the anti-Semitic *L'Action Française*, led by Léon Daudet, son of the novelist Alphonse Daudet, despite the fact that Marie was formally a Catholic.

All of this gives Albert a close insight into the personality and strength needed as a victim of public abuse. He's sympathetic, intrigued and in no small measure enchanted by her courage.

Langevin also enchants him. The imposing physicist, with his handlebar moustache, militaristic bearing and slim, tall figure, published a popular explanation of relativity in 1911: 'L'evolution de l'espace et du temps' in *Scientia*.

At the Solvay Conference, Albert learns that Marie has become embroiled in an affair with Langevin, who's five years her junior, married and the father of four children with his wife, Jeanne. She has long been suspicious of her husband's relationship with Marie and hires a detective to search his desk at the Sorbonne. The detective finds a series of love letters from Marie to Langevin and turns them over to *L'Action Française*. Extracts from the letters are published in the French press.

Jeanne prepares legal action to gain custody of her four children. The scandal grips France.

The Swedish Academy tells Marie not to go to Stockholm to receive the prize, to which Marie replies: 'I believe there is no connection between my scientific work and the facts of my private life.'

Albert takes a sanguine view: 'She is an unpretentious, honest person with a sparkling intelligence. Despite her passionate nature, she is not attractive enough to represent a danger to anyone.'

Early in November the delegates go their separate ways.

Albert writes to Marie:

Highly esteemed Mrs Curie,

Do not laugh at me for writing you without having anything sensible to say. But I am so enraged by the base manner in which the public is presently daring to concern itself with you that I absolutely must give vent to this feeling. However, I am convinced that you consistently despise this rabble, whether it obsequiously lavishes respect on you or whether it attempts to satiate its lust for sensationalism! I am impelled to tell you how much I have come to admire your intellect, your drive, and your honesty, and that I consider myself lucky to have made your personal acquaintance in Brussels. Anyone who does not number among these reptiles is certainly happy, now as before, that we have such personages among us as you, and Langevin too, real people with whom one feels privileged to be in contact. If the rabble continues to occupy itself with you, then simply don't read that hogwash, but rather leave it to the reptile for whom it has been fabricated.

With most amicable regards to you, Langevin, and Perrin, yours very truly,

A. Einstein

PS I have determined the statistical law of motion of the diatomic molecule in Planck's radiation field by means of a comical witticism, naturally under the constraint that the structure's motion follows the law of standard mechanics. My hope that this law is valid in reality is very small, though.

Albert is fascinated and flattered by the approaches he receives from institutions offering him appointments and opportunities to lecture. When he returns to Prague he and Mileva decide to travel to Zürich to see if the ETH will give him an appointment. They are shocked to find that education officials in Zürich declare that the appointment of a professor in theoretical physics is an extravagance.

Heinrich Zangger speaks up in support of Albert: 'He is not a good teacher for mentally lazy gentlemen who merely want to fill a notebook and then learn it by heart for an exam; he is not a smooth talker but anyone wishing to learn honestly how to develop his ideas in physics in an honest way, from deep within, and how to examine a premise carefully and see the pitfalls and the problems in his reflections, will find Einstein a first class teacher, because of all that is expressed in his lectures, which force the audience to think along.'

Zangger is outraged by the manoeuvring in Zürich.

Albert writes to Zangger: 'Leave the Polytechnic to God's inscrutable ways.'

He doesn't give up. He enlists Marie Curie and Poincaré to write recommendations. This does the trick. The ETH appoints Albert Professor of Theoretical Physics. Albert, Mileva and the children are happy to be returning to Zürich.

The Prague newspapers take the news of Albert's departure badly, suggesting that anti-Semitism may have influenced Albert's departure. Albert publically denies it. He fights to control the hurt.

Yet again they pack their belongings and travel the 640 kilometres back to Zürich.

There they move into a six-room apartment, his fifth home in Zürich. Albert resumes his regular meetings with Zangger and Grossmann. With Mileva and the boys in tow, he attends Sunday musical evenings at the mathematician Adolf Hurwitz's house. They play Mozart and, to Mileva's delight, Schumann.

Albert may be in his element. But it escapes no one's attention, least of all Albert's, that Mileva's physical and mental state is declining. The bitter winter offers her no solace.

ALBERT AND HIS BELOVED ELSA

More than ever in demand to answer questions, Albert takes a trip to Berlin to discuss quantum photochemistry with Emil Gabriel Warburg at the Physikalisch-Technische Reichsanstalt. Walther Nernst is keen to discuss issues involving specific heat: the amount of heat per unit of mass required to raise the temperature by one degree Celsius, and Fritz Haber wants to ask Albert questions about quantum chemistry.

He stays with Warburg and catches up with his family: Aunt Fanny and Uncle Rudolf, son of Raphael Einstein, a brother of Albert's paternal grandfather. Elsa, Fanny's daughter and Albert's second cousin, is in Berlin too, staying with her parents in Schöneberg, in the southern outskirts.

The sight of Elsa takes Albert back to the early days in Munich. Three years Albert's senior, she is now divorced from the textile merchant Max Löwenthal, with whom she has two daughters: bashful Margot, eleven; and headstrong Ilse, nine. With fine blonde hair and short-sighted, vivid blue eyes, Elsa is warm-hearted and, having changed her name back to Einstein, has become something of a figure in artistic, political and scientific circles.

They take the S-Bahn to the Grosser Wannsee and the Kleiner Wannsee lakes on the Havel River. They buy sherbet, watch the sailing boats criss-crossing the shimmering water.

'I am so lonely. I am unloved. I just want someone I can trust. Who understands everything in my heart and mind. Can you understand?'

'Yes, dearest Albert.'

They book into the Hotel Bonverde.

He stoops down, picks a flower and holds it out to Elsa. 'For you.'

'For me?'

'For you.'

'What is it?'

'*Myosotis alpestris*. It's a forget-me-not. Promise me?'

'Anything.'

'Forget me not.'

She draws his mouth to hers and they kiss.

Albert sees the face of Mileva from sixteen years before.

'You want me for ever?' Elsa says.

'Yes.'

Her perfume arouses him.

She whispers in her ear: 'I am with you.'

'"The setting sun sets stars up over me."'

'That's beautiful,' she says. 'Did you think of that for your naughty little Elsa?'

'I thought of it. Goethe wrote it. We are both poor devils. Each chained to ruthless duties. I'd be very happy just to walk a few steps at your side or have pleasure some other way in your presence.'

*

Albert is helpless in his confusion.

A fortnight later he changes his mind and writes to her from Zürich: 'I am writing to you today for the last time and submitting myself to the inevitable, and you must do the same. You know it is not hardness of heart or lack of feeling that makes me talk like this, because you know that, like you, I bear my cross without hope. If you ever have a hard time or otherwise feel the need to confide in somebody, then remember you have a cousin who will feel for you no matter what the issue might be.'

Elsa picks up the signal. She's the one Albert needs as confidante.

She buys a postcard and sprays it with Kölnisch Wasser, knowing the perfume will remind him of her body in his bed.

ELSA'S POSTCARD

On a separate sheet of paper she carefully writes out Goethe's love poem.

Nearness of the Beloved

I think of you when sunlight on the ocean
   Glimmers at noon;
I think of you when shimmers in the river
   Mirror the moon.

I see you in the rise of dust that covers
   The distant ridge,
In each deep midnight where the wanderer quivers
   On the high bridge,

I hear you in the low and muffled rustle
   Of rolling seas.
I often go to quiet groves and listen
   To things at peace.

I am with you. However far you are,
   I know you're near!
Oh what I'd give, as sun gives way to star,
   To have you here.

MAX PLANCK

WALTHER NERNST

Albert spends the summer in Zürich at 116 Hofstrasse, a grandiose building with views of the lake and the Alps. The family takes trips on the paddle-steamer *Stadt Rapperswil*, built by Escher, Wyss & C. for the Zürich-Schifffahrtsgesellschaft. He gazes at the smoke rising from its snub funnel like the smoke from his pipe.

He's buoyed up by the news that he's been given the rare honour, second only to the Nobel Prize, of election to the Prussian Academy of Sciences. And honoured still more when Max Planck and Walther Nernst arrive in Zürich on a mission to persuade Albert to move to Berlin. They know of Albert's misgivings about Germany. To get him to accept their invitation will be tough.

Albert meets Planck and Nernst at Zürich's Hauptbahnhof and takes them to the ETH.

Albert sits at his desk puffing on his pipe.

Nernst lights a cigarette and announces with Prussian gravity: 'Without being boastful' – which is what he is – 'I have the ear of the Kaiser. We both recognise the need for science and technology to boost the nation's economy. The Kaiser has enthusiastically given his approval to the foundation of several research institutes: the Kaiser Wilhelm Foundation for the Advancement of Science. Germany's aim is to become an economic world power for the nation's benefit.'

'Nation's benefit . . .' says Albert. 'Don't you, rather, mean for the benefit of the monarch?'

Nernst flinches. 'I wouldn't put it quite like that.'

'Tell me,' says Albert, 'who are the shining lights of the Kaiser Wilhelm Foundation for the Advancement of Science?'

The tall, spare Planck chimes in: 'The Prussian minister for religious, educational and medical affairs, August Bodo Wilhelm Clemens Paul von Trott zu Solz, is chairman.'

'You will need a large chair to accommodate a man with such an enormous name.'

'Trott zu Solz belongs to a noble family, a member of the Hessian Protestant Uradel and the Old Hessian Knighthood, descended from the thirteenth century. The family seat is in Solz and they have a castle in Imshausen. They're imperial barons.'

'The Einsteins do not require a family seat,' Albert says. 'I speak to everyone in the same way.'

The visitors give hollow chuckles.

'Trott zu Solz chaired the first meeting of eighty-three voting members, including Gustav Krupp von Bohlen und Halbach, the banker Ludwig Delbrück and the industrialist Henry Theodore von Böttinger. Fritz Haber was also there. You know Haber?'

'Very ambitious,' says Albert.

'Yes. Wilhelm II awarded a clunking chain of office to Adolf von Harnack, the president of his society. You know of von Harnack?'

'I know the library in Berlin.'

'You know of its holdings?'

'The fifth-century Quedlinburg Itala fragment. A Gutenberg

Bible. Goethe's letters. The biggest collection of manuscripts of J.S. Bach and my beloved Mozart.'

'And the original score of Beethoven's Symphony No. 9.'

'I know. I am more interested in Mozart.'

'Truly wonderful,' Nernst says jovially.

'The Beethoven score?' says Albert.

'That, yes,' says Nernst. 'And members wear ribbons with the Kaiser's portrait woven in orange silk in their buttonholes. Members of senate attend ceremonies in flowing green robes with red collars, gold buttons and medals.'

'Very colourful,' says Albert.

'Our first offer to you,' says Planck, 'is a research professorship at the University of Berlin funded by Geheimrat Leopold Koppel, the entrepreneur who founded the private banking house Koppel und Co. and the industrial firms Auergesellschaft, OSRAM, and the philanthropic foundation, the Koppel-Stiftung.'

'How kind,' says Albert.

'The second offer is the directorship of a new Kaiser Wilhelm Institute devoted to physics to be founded shortly. What do you think?'

'It's very flattering. Thank you, gentlemen.'

'The intellectual climate is perfect,' Nernst says.

'The salary is good,' Planck adds.

'You won't have to lecture,' Nernst says.

'What do you think of the future?' asks Planck.

'I never think of the future. It comes soon enough. I will consult my wife. And I will let you know my decision.'

Now if Mileva were to stay in Zürich, there's Elsa in Berlin. Juggling principles is his forte. Juggling women isn't. This is a problem of his own making.

'You hate Prussia,' Mileva says.

'Yes, but at least we'll be free of financial worries.'

'We will?'

'And I'll be free from administrative duties.'

'You will?'

'I'll be free to work.'

'And me?' Mileva asks.

'You'll be happy in Berlin.'

'How do you know?'

'You'll be honoured as my wife.'

'Albert, don't you understand what I'm saying – I want to be honoured as Mileva Maric.'

'Then why not go to Berlin and choose a really fine apartment for us – a place that will do honour and credit to Mileva Maric?'

'What honour do I have left? I am Frau Einstein. I am no more "Mileva Maric". The whole world knows who you are. And me?'

Albert is silent. He lights his pipe.

'But me?' Mileva says. 'Who am I?'

'I know who you are,' says Albert. He flaps away a cloud of pipe smoke.

'That's not enough,' Mileva shouts. 'It's time you told me the truth.'

'About what?'

'Your mistress.'

Albert fiddles with his pipe in silence.

'You are avoiding my eyes,' Mileva says.

He tilts his head and blinks.

'Are you going to tell me?'

He takes a long slow breath.

'Why are you silent?'

He sits very still, the pipe smoke curling away from his open mouth.

'Well?'

'I love you,' he says. 'I love you.'

'And this woman?'

He puts his hand over his mouth and shuffles his feet.

Mileva opens a crumpled piece of paper. Handing it to Albert, she says: 'Read it.'

Albert reads his own handwriting: 'How was I able to live alone before, my little everything? Without you I lack self-confidence, passion for work, and enjoyment of life – in short, without you, my life is no life.'

'That's true,' says Albert.

'And Elsa?'

'What about her?'

'Do you love her?'

'No.'

'You share her bed?'

Albert is silent.

'Elsa!' Mileva shouts. 'She's a bitch.'

Albert writes to Elsa:

I have to have someone to love, otherwise life is miserable. And this someone is you; you cannot do anything about it, since I am not asking you for permission. I am the absolute ruler in the netherworld of my imagination, or at least that is what I choose to think. How nice it would be if we could share in managing a small bohemian household. My wife whines incessantly to me about Berlin and her fear of the relatives. She feels persecuted and is afraid that the end of March will see her last peaceful days. Well, there is some truth in this. My mother is otherwise good-natured, but she is a really fiendish mother-in-law. When she stays with us the air is full of dynamite.

Fear is never far away.

I shudder at the thought of seeing her and *you* together. She will writhe like a worm if she sees you even from afar! I treat my wife as an employee whom I cannot fire. I have my own bedroom and avoid being alone with her. She is an unfriendly humourless creature who has nothing from life herself and smothers the joy in life of others through her mere presence.

With the patient help of the Habers, Mileva finds a suitable apartment at the corner of Ehrenbergstrasse 33 in Dahlem and Rudeloffweg, not far from the Institute.

Despite any lingering misgivings he may have about Berlin, Albert heads there in March. Mileva takes the children to a health spa in Ticino in Switzerland.

Anxious and lonely, Albert stays with his uncle Jakob on Wilmersdorferstrasse, where his mother is looking after domestic arrangements. Elsa is waiting for him.

'You must decide what you want of her,' Elsa tells him, her blue eyes smiling.

So Albert does what Elsa suggests and prepares a list of conditions to be met by Mileva if they are to continue to live together as man and wife.

A. You make sure:
1. That my clothes and laundry are kept in good order and repair.
2. That I receive my three meals regularly in my room.
3. That my bedroom and office are always kept neat, in particular that the desk is available <u>to me alone</u>.

B. You renounce all personal relations with me as far as maintaining them is not absolutely required for social reasons. Specifically, you do without:

1. My sitting at home with you.

2. My going out or travelling together with you.

C. In your relations with me you commit yourself explicitly to adhering to the following points:

1. You are neither to expect intimacy from me nor to reproach me in any way.

2. You must desist immediately from addressing me, if I request it.

3. You must leave my bedroom or office immediately without protest if I so request.

D. You commit yourself not to disparage me either in words or in deed in my front of my children.

'Well?'

Mileva stares at him in silence.

Albert fiddles with his pipe. 'I am only interested in my children, in Albertli and Tete.'

'You call them *your* children?' she yells.

'They are my sons,' Albert says meekly.

'They are *my* sons. Tete is not well. He needs a proper father.'

'He has me.'

'I am his mother. How can you give me this thing – this list?'

'It will mend our marriage.'

'It will not.'

'Then we must separate,' Albert says.

'How will I live?'

'On half my income,' Albert says. 'On 5,600 marks a year.'

'I see, Albert,' she says, enraged. 'If that's what you want.'

'So be it.'

'It's cruel, Albert. You are cruel. Cruel beyond belief.'

Albert accompanies Mileva, Albertli and Tete to the Anhalter Bahnhof and sees them on the train to Zürich.

He breaks down and sobs without cease.

'You commit a crime against our children and you cry like a baby,' Mileva says.

'Will you change your mind?' he begs her.

'No.'

'It is in such times that we see to what a miserable species of cattle we belong.'

She glares at him in silence.

Still weeping, Albert leaves the station through its main exit – a triumphal arch – in defeat: out onto the newly built Bahnhofstrasse, his eyes stinging.

Their marriage has lasted eleven years and they have spent eighteen years as a couple. The relationship, like the building little Albert had constructed out of playing cards, lies in a chaotic heap. A symbol of foreboding as Europe disintegrates.

SARAJEVO

In Sarajevo, a nineteen-year-old tubercular Bosnian Serb, Gavrilo Princip, plans to assassinate Archduke Franz Ferdinand, heir presumptive to the throne of the Austro-Hungarian Empire.

The imperial motorcade of six open-topped cars approaches City Hall. In the front car is the mayor of Sarajevo and the city's commissioner of police. Franz Ferdinand and his wife, Sophie, Duchess of Hohenberg, are in the second car with Oskar Potiorek, Governor of Bosnia and Herzegovina and inspector general of the Austro-Hungarian army, and Count Franz von Harrach, who is riding on the running board, serving as a bodyguard to the archduke. The first shot fails to kill him. Princip panics and flees. A second terrorist throws a bomb at the motorcade. The bomb explodes injuring people in the crowd. With Franz Ferdinand unhurt, the motorcade speeds off and the police detain the bomb-thrower.

After the reception in City Hall, General Potiorek begs Franz Ferdinand to leave the city. The archduke is understandably furious about the assassination attempt. He insists upon visiting the wounded.

The officials persuade the archduke to take the shortest route out of the city. The motorcade makes a sharp turn at the bridge over the River Miljacka, slowing down to make the turn. Princip is waiting with his blowback-operated, semi-automatic FN Model 1910 Browning pistol, manufactured by Fabrique Nationale in Belgium. Princip steps off the kerb, draws his Browning from his coat and fires two shots from a distance of five feet.

The first shot hits the pregnant Archduchess Sophie in the stomach.

The Archduke screams out: 'Sophie, Sophie, don't die. Live for my children.'

The second bullet hits the Archduke close to the heart.

Potsdamer Platz is the social hub of Berlin, where Albert and Elsa gossip over coffee in the Hotel Esplanade, the Hotel Excelsior or the Hotel Piccadilly, now renamed Café Vaterland a mere two weeks into the war. Ladies in vast feathered hats walk arm-in-arm. The shabby and the chic chatter and laugh.

Albert and Elsa read their favourite newspaper, *Berliner Tageblatt*. Albert's moods are dark. 'Why this insane German predilection for territorial conquest?'

'It'll all be over in a few weeks,' Elsa says.

'Germany's appetite for territorial conquest is alarming enough, but its reputation for brutality and violence is nothing short of damning. The Kaiserreich's record abroad is inhumane even by contemporary standards.'

They stroll through the streets, carefully avoiding the horse-drawn brewery drays and the Maybach limousines.

'Europe in its madness is embarking on something incredibly preposterous,' Albert announces. 'I feel pity and disgust.'

'There's nothing we can do,' says Elsa.

Kottbusser Strasse leads them to the canal and they explore the market stalls in the Maybachufer: buying red cabbage, goat fat and kippered herring. Bottles of essence of lily of the valley.

They joke with the Italian selling plaster statues at the Landwehr Canal bridge. They haggle with the second-hand booksellers in the Scheunenviertel.

'Nernst is fifty. He's volunteered as an ambulance driver.'

'That's noble of him,' says Elsa.

'And Planck, in the name of God, says: "It's a great feeling to be able to call oneself a German."'

'You are Swiss.'

'Thank the Lord,' says Albert. 'It gets even worse. Planck, in his nationalistic fever, has joined Nernst, Röntgen and Wien in signing an Appeal to the Cultured World. Look. It's in the *Berliner Tageblatt.*'

He reads aloud to Elsa:

As representatives of German Science and Art, we hereby protest to the civilised world against the lies and calumnies with which our enemies are endeavouring to stain the honour of Germany in her hard struggle for existence – in a struggle that has been forced on her.

It is not true that Germany is guilty of having caused this war. Neither the people, Government, nor the Kaiser wanted war. Germany did her utmost to prevent it; for this assertion the world has documental proof. Often enough during the twenty-six years of his reign has Wilhelm II shown himself to be the upholder of peace, and often enough has this fact been acknowledged by our opponents. Nay, even the Kaiser, whom they now dare to call an Attila, has been ridiculed by them for years, because of his steadfast endeavours to maintain universal peace. Not till a numerical superiority which has been lying in wait on the frontiers assailed us did the whole nation rise to a man.

It is not true that we trespassed in neutral Belgium. It has been proved that France and England had resolved on such a trespass, and it has likewise been proved that Belgium had agreed to their doing so. It would have been suicide on our part not to have preempted this.

It is not true that the life and property of a single Belgian citizen was injured by our soldiers without the bitterest self-defence having made it necessary; for again and again, notwithstanding repeated threats, the citizens lay in ambush, shooting at the troops out of the houses, mutilating the wounded, and murdering in cold blood the medical men while they were doing their Samaritan work. There can be no baser abuse than the suppression of these crimes with the view of letting the Germans appear to be criminals only for having justly punished these assassins for their wicked deeds.

It is not true that our troops treated Louvain brutally. Furious inhabitants having treacherously fallen upon them in their quarters, our troops with aching hearts were obliged to set fire to a part of the town as a punishment. The greatest part of Louvain has been preserved. The famous Town Hall stands quite intact; for at great self-sacrifice our soldiers saved it from destruction by the flames. Every German would of course greatly regret if, in the course of this terrible war, any works of art should have been destroyed or be destroyed at some future time, but inasmuch as in our great love for art we cannot be surpassed by any other nation, in the same degree we must decidedly refuse to buy a German defeat at the cost of saving a work of art.

It is not true that our warfare pays no respect to international laws. It knows no undisciplined cruelty. But in the east the earth is saturated with the blood of women and children unmercifully butchered by the wild Russian troops, and in the west dumdum bullets mutilate the breasts of our soldiers. Those who have allied themselves with Russians and Serbians, and present such a shameful scene to the world as that of inciting Mongolians and negroes against the white race, have no right whatever to call themselves upholders of civilisation.

It is not true that the combat against our so-called militarism is not a combat against our civilisation as our enemies hypocritically pretend it is. Were it not for German militarism, German civilisation would long since have been extirpated. For its protection it arose in a land which for centuries had been plagued by bands of robbers as no other land had been. The German Army and the German people are one and today this consciousness fraternises 70 million Germans, all ranks, positions, and parties being one.

We cannot wrest the poisonous weapon – the lie – out of the hands of our enemies. All we can do is to proclaim to all the world that our enemies are giving false witness against us. You, who know us, who with us have protected the most holy possessions of man, we call to you:

Have faith in us! Believe, that we shall carry on this war to the end as a civilised nation, to whom the legacy of a Goethe, a Beethoven, and a Kant is just as sacred as its own hearths and homes.

For this we pledge you our names and our honour.

Elsa listens intently to the grandiloquence.

They explore the *Kiez*, the *Miljöh*, and the old, genuine Berlin.

'All this will be swept away,' Albert says. 'Look. This neighbourhood is the Berlin of we Jews, of Poles and Russians from the East, enjoying the Jewish street culture. Listen to the music of the radios and gramophones, barrel-organs and street-singers. Is this to be destroyed by madness?'

GEORG FRIEDRICH NICOLAI

Albert soon finds a like-minded protester in the pacifist physiologist Georg Friedrich Nicolai, doctor-friend of Elsa.

Nicolai is egocentric, sexually voracious. He's been thrown out of boarding schools and colleges for brawling, duelling and fathering illegitimate children. He has lived variously in Paris and in Leipzig, where he was a drama critic, travelled in Asia and worked in St Petersburg with Ivan Pavlov, the physiologist who won the Nobel Prize in Medicine in 1904, becoming the first Russian Nobel laureate. Nicolai became medical director of the Second Medical Clinic of the Charité Hospital in Berlin. In 1910, together with his superior Friedrich Kraus, he published a fundamental textbook of electrocardiography. He's now cardiologist to the royal family and works in a military hospital.

Nicolai can see that armaments will matter far more than courage or military know-how. He writes a 'Manifesto to the Europeans'. It marks Albert's beginning as a political activist of consequence.

'Manifesto to the Europeans'

Through technology the world has become *smaller*, the *states* of the large peninsula of Europe appear today as close to each other as the cities of each small Mediterranean peninsula appeared in ancient times. In the needs and experiences of every individual, based on his awareness of manifold of relations, Europe – one could almost say the world – already outlines itself as an element of unity.

It would consequently be a duty of the educated and well-meaning European to at least make the attempt to prevent Europe – on account of its deficient organisation as a whole – from suffering the same tragic fate as ancient Greece once did. Should Europe too gradually exhaust itself and thus perish from fratricidal war?

The struggle raging today will likely produce no victor; it will leave probably only the vanquished. Therefore, it seems not only *good*, but rather bitterly *necessary that educated men of all nations* marshal their influence such that – whatever the still uncertain end of the war may be – the *terms of peace shall not become the wellspring of future wars.* The evident fact that through this war all European relational conditions slipped into an *unstable and plasticised state* should rather be used to create an organic European whole. The technological and intellectual conditions for this are extant . . . the time has come when *Europe must act as one in order to protect her soil, her inhabitants, and her culture.*

To this end, it seems first of all to be a necessity that all those who have a place in their heart for European culture and civilisation, in other words, those who can be called in *Goethe's* prescient words '*good Europeans*', come together. To this end we only want to urge and appeal; and if you feel as we do, if you are like-mindedly determined to *provide Europe with the farthest-reaching possible resonance,* then we ask you to please send your (supporting) signature to us.

To their bitter disappointment, of the 100 intellectuals Albert and Nicolai approach, they can muster only two co-signatories: the astronomer Wilhelm Julius Foerster and the philosopher Otto Buek.

No one in Berlin will publish the manifesto. So Nicolai disseminates it privately and resorts to giving anti-war lectures to his classes. The public ignores 'The Manifesto to the Europeans'. When the government hears about it, Nicolai is sacked from his position as cardiologist to the German royal family, stripped of his professorship at the University of Berlin and his post at the Charité Hospital, and is farmed out as a garrison physician in Grudziądz, south of Gdansk. There he passes the time fox-hunting with his camp commandant.

*

105

In August 1915, Albert receives an invitation that will expand his circle of pacifist protesters. The liberal politician Walther Schücking invites Albert to join the *Bund Neues Vaterland*, Association for a New Fatherland. It has four main goals: 'Building understanding among nations. Abolition of domination of power based upon class. Cooperation in the realisation of socialism. Developing the culture of personality. Educating youth in pacifism.'

'Here's something I can go along with,' Albert tells Elsa. 'The government can't ignore these people.'

'Who are they?' Elsa asks.

He calls out the names of the pacifist luminaries with increasing delight. 'Kurt von Tepper-Laski's an equestrian and journalist. Hugo Simon helped found the bank Bett, Carsh, Simon & Co. With his wife, Gertrud, he's turned his house on Drakestrasse into a veritable centre for art and culture, frequented by writers and intellectuals such as Heinrich and Thomas Mann, René Schikele, Stefan Zweig, Harry Kessler, Walther Rathenau, Kurt Tucholsky, Jakob Wassermann, maestro Bruno Walter, Walter Benjamin and artists of the avant-garde.'

'It's wonderful, Albert. Some good comes out of war.'

'None, Elsa. None.'

The government doesn't ignore the luminaries. With surprising naivety members lobby contacts in the Reichstag. The result is that the police conduct surveillance operations against them.

The High Command of the Official Seals threatens to close it.

Secretary Lilli Jannasch is sent to prison. After a demonstration against the war in Berlin, Karl Liebknecht is sentenced to two and a half years in prison for high treason. In court he shouts: '*Nieder mit dem Krieg! Nieder mit der Regierung!*' 'Down with the war! Down with the government!' His sentence is increased to four years and one month.

*

If the wind outside blows, if the house of cards trembles, then close the shutters and improve the foundations of the house. That's roughly the line Albert takes.

'I am living a very secluded and yet not lonely life,' he writes to Zangger, who's in Zürich. 'Thanks to the loving care of my cousin, who had drawn me to Berlin in the first place, of course. I shall never give up the state of living alone which has manifested itself as an indescribable blessing.'

The three-room apartment is at Wittelsbacherstraße 13 in a well-to-do neighbourhood near Fehrbelliner Platz. He has a telephone number, Berlin 2807. The apartment is bare except for overflowing bookshelves. Here he works long hours alone on the general theory of relativity. Again he writes to Zangger: 'My human and professional contacts are few but very harmonious and rewarding, my public life withdrawn and simple. I must say that to me I seem one of the happiest of persons.'

As for Elsa, he writes to Besso of 'the extremely agreeable, really fine relationship with my cousin, the permanent nature of which is guaranteed by a renunciation of marriage'. And that in spite of the fact he's already told her he would marry her.

This year. Next year. Some time. Whenever.

Behind the shutters of the Wittelsbacherstraße apartment he works without cease, to the limits of his physical and mental powers. The work exhausts him. He's plagued by stomach pain, falls ill with jaundice, stomach ulcers, then gallstones. His pain is constant and most violent when he goes to the toilet or passes wind or is throwing up. It's triggered by eating fatty foods and occurs at any time, waking him during the night.

In two months he loses fifty-six pounds.

ANOTHER OF ELSA'S FANCIFUL POSTCARDS

Elsa persuades him to move into a spacious fourth-floor apartment at Haberlandstrasse 5, near hers. She feeds him, makes love to him, nurtures him back to strength.

She shows him the new costume she's bought.

'Come to Mama, who'll make you happy.'

He tells Elsa that Haber's warned him: 'We must be dreadfully careful so that we, i.e., you do not become the subject of idle gossip. Do not go out alone. Haber will inform Planck so that my nearest colleagues do not first hear about the matter from rumours. You will have to perform wonders of tact and restraint so that you are not looked upon as a kind of murderess; appearances are very much against us.'

Now she's his constant companion, nursing him back to health, Elsa wants to put the relationship on a more permanent footing.

TETE, MILEVA AND HANS ALBERT

Hans Albert keeps up a regular correspondence with his father.

He says that Tete dreams that Papa's with them. He describes the progress of his piano playing: sonatas by Haydn and Mozart. He sends Albert a sketch of a model sailing ship he's carving in wood.

Albert replies:

My dear little Albert,

Yesterday I received your dear letter and was very happy with it. I was already afraid you wouldn't write to me at all any more. You told me when I was in Zürich, that it is awkward for you when I come to Zürich. Therefore I think it is better if we get together in a different place, where nobody will interfere with our comfort. I will in any case urge that each year we spend a whole month together, so that you see that you have a father who is fond of you and who loves you. You can also learn many good and beautiful things from me, something another cannot as easily offer you. What I have achieved through such a lot of strenuous work shall not only be there for strangers but especially for my own boys. These days I have completed one of the most beautiful works of my life, when you are bigger, I will tell you about it.

I am very pleased that you find joy with the piano. This and carpentry are in my opinion for your age the best pursuits, better even than school. Because those are things which fit a young person such as you very well. Mainly play the things on the piano, which please you, even if the teacher does not assign those. That is the way to learn the most, that when you are doing something with such enjoyment that you don't notice that the time passes. I am sometimes so wrapped up in my work that I forget about the noon meal . . .

Be with Tete kissed by your

Papa

Soon after, Mileva suffers a nervous breakdown and is confined in the Zürich Theodosianum Parkseite Klinik. The boys are placed in the care of a housekeeper.

Money is hard to come by, because Albert's payment transfers to Switzerland are frequently delayed.

Hans Albert is left to take care of himself when Mileva and Tete are confined in the Bethanien Klinik in Zürich – Mileva with chronic nerve pressure on her spine; Tete with inflamed lungs. Hans Albert is himself hospitalised and then taken in by the Zangger family. Albert is cast down. He fears for the mental and physical state of all of them. His one sanctuary is work.

Elsa begs him to slow up. He won't. He thinks of issuing a public demand for the division and subjugation of Germany and its destruction. He restrains himself with difficulty. Elsa wonders what he's talking about. Albert admits he's sometimes not sure himself.

Early in November 1915, he organises enough material for the first of his four lectures on the general theory of relativity that he's wrestled with for eight years.

ENTRANCE TO GRAND LECTURE HALL

On 25 November 1915, in the grand lecture hall of the Prussian Academy of Sciences, Unter den Linden 8, Berlin, Albert asks:

Do we require a new theory of gravitation given that Newtonian physics has served us so well for two hundred and fifty years and seems to explain everything?

Newton's gravity is action at a distance. Two bodies, the earth and moon for example, are joined as if by invisible threads. How is the mechanism by which the force is transmitted? Newton's formulae leave us with the idea that gravity reaches another body – no matter how far away – instantaneously. This is contradicted by my special theory of relativity. I maintain that no physical effect can spread faster than the speed of light.

Gravity is different. It's a property of space and time. Matter bends space. Space forces matter to describe specific motions. The moon orbits the earth because the earth and the moon distort space. Gravity is uniquely a property of space-time geometry. Other natural forces act within space and time. So what is gravitation. It is space and time. This is my general theory of relativity. Thus, the general theory of relativity as a logical edifice has finally been completed.

The once sceptical Max von Laue writes that curved space 'is by no means a mathematical construct but a reality that is inherent in all physical processes. This discovery is Albert Einstein's greatest achievement.' Max Born describes it as 'the greatest feat of human thinking about nature, the most amazing combination of philosophical penetration, physical intuition and mathematical skill'.

Albert has worked out how the Sun makes an invisible pull on Earth from a distance of 93 million miles through empty space. The only thing that could be doing the pulling is the only thing out there: space itself. The matter that is Sun and Earth causes space to bend.

Time can bend too. The closer a clock is to a massive body like Earth, the slower it ticks. Space and time are woven into one continuum called space-time. Events taking place at the one time for one person can take place at a different time for another.

Albert is euphoric. He declares to his friends that the theory is one of 'incomparable beauty'. He tells Sommerfeld that it's 'the most momentous discovery I've made in my life'.

His euphoria soon diminishes when chaotic family problems engulf him.

Albert had planned to see Hans Albert. His son, now eleven years old, says he doesn't want to see his father. 'The unkind tone of your letter dismays me very much,' he tells Hans Albert. 'I see that my visit would bring you little joy, therefore I think it's wrong to sit in a train for two hours and 20 minutes.'

There was an unpleasantness about Albert's Christmas present to his son. Mileva had bought skis for the boy costing 70 francs. Hans Albert tells his father that Mileva bought them on condition Albert contribute, to which Albert replied: 'I do think that a luxury gift costing 70 francs does not match our modest circumstances.'

Finally, Albert decides to go to Zürich. He tells Mileva: 'There is a faint chance that I'll please little Albert by coming.'

Albert shows no immediate sign of recovering from exhaustion. This, along with the problems of crossing the German border, scupper the plans for the Christmas visit. Albert says he will make a visit the following Easter.

'The role as the wife of a genius is never easy,' Besso writes to Albert. Besso encourages Albert to remember that Mileva evinces 'not only meanness but goodness'.

Before realising the plan to see his children, Albert sets about trying to persuade Mileva to agree to a divorce. He explains that Elsa's reputation is being trashed by rumours of her relationship with him.' 'This weighs on me,' he tells Mileva '. . . and ought to be redressed by formal marriage. Try to imagine yourself in my position for once.'

He goes to Zürich, sees Hans but not Mileva, who shuts the door in his face. A few months later she is bedridden with a heart problem.

Besso and Zangger again try to calm matters. To which Albert replies that Mileva is leading them down the garden path. 'You have no idea of the natural craftiness of such a woman.'

Besso, understandably, finds Albert's opinions unacceptable. One effect is that Hans Albert stops writing to his father.

Albert inevitably finds solace in his scientific work, publishing *Relativity: The Special and the General Theory*. He reads it to Elsa's daughter Margot, who doesn't let on that she simply doesn't understand a word of it.

He approaches Mileva a second time about divorce, offering more money, and the extraordinary notion that if he one day receives the Nobel Prize, the money will be given to Mileva. This will amount to 135,000 Swedish kronor. She initially dismisses the idea. Then she changes her mind. She's ill and weak. Tete is in a sanatorium. Mileva's sister is in an asylum. Her brother has been taken prisoner by the Russians.

Albert tries and fails to answer the question, which will come first: the end of the war or the end of his marriage?

The war is one thing. The war with Mileva is another. Yet another is the increasing anti-Semitism in the German scientific establishment overshadowing his life and diminishing his buoyancy.

The Reichshammerbund (the Reich Hammer League) disgusts him. Founded by Theodor Fritsch, it declares that the Jews have contaminated Germany. Their declarations, they reason, have their basis in biology. It seeks to bring together anti-Semitic organisations to renew the German way of life. Its sign is the swastika. Fritsch establishes a more secretive network of anti-Semites, the Germanenorden, a group of occultists and freemasons. The Reichshammerbund and Germanenorden welcome war as the chance to banish softness from Germany and re-establish discipline and militarism, demanding that Germans should concentrate on *Deutsche Physik* not Jewish physics.

Albert's conspicuous loss of weight distresses Elsa. She calls in the doctor, who advises a diet of pasta, rice and sweetened rusks like Melba toast.

Elsa finds him eggs, butter and goat's milk. All this in spite of the worsening food shortages. She has well-off friends who've filled their gardens with chickens and planted vegetables. In the absence of potatoes she cooks turnips, making them palatable with supplies of scarce sugar. She even manages, no matter what the doctor says, to buy the occasional goose, an almost unobtainable luxury. Albert is delighted with her cooking, and her housekeeping skills she exercises with discretion so he isn't disturbed. So very different from Mileva.

The nation's food woes are a constant topic of debate among Elsa's friends.

'Everyone is blaming we Jews,' she says to Albert. 'They blame it on the influx of Jewish refugees from the East. They see us as middle-men: *Geschäftsjude*.'

'We are to blame for everything?' Albert says.

'That's what they say.'

'I am German,' says Albert. 'You are German. My first language is German. We live in Berlin. The state to which I belong as a citizen plays not the slightest role in my emotional life. I regard a person's relations with the state as a business matter, rather like one's relations with a life assurance company.'

'Why – why do they hate us?'

'Jews make the perfect scapegoat for any country experiencing extreme social, economic, or political difficulties. The reason for this is two-fold. First of all, there's hardly a country in the world that does not have a Jewish element in the population. And secondly, wherever Jews live, they are a minority of the population, and a small minority at that, so that they are not powerful enough to defend themselves against a mass attack. It is very easy for governments to divert attention from their own mistakes by blaming Jews for this or that political theory, such as communism or socialism.'

'I heard a man accusing us of starting the war.'

'Nothing new in that. Throughout history, Jews have been accused of all sorts of treachery, such as poisoning water wells or murdering children as religious sacrifices. Much of this can be attributed to jealousy, because, despite the fact that Jewish people have always been thinly populated in various countries, they have always had a disproportionate number of outstanding public figures.'

'It frightens me, Albertli.'

'I will protect you, my beloved. Germany is the best place for me to live and work.'

'What about Switzerland?'

'And return to Zürich where we'll be near Mileva?'

'You remain a pacifist?'

'I remain a pacifist.'

Which is difficult for him to do when he learns of Zyklon B.

FRITZ HABER

Albert's friend Haber, director of the Kaiser Wilhelm Institute for Physical Chemistry, pledges that his laboratory will serve the Deutsches Kaiserreich.

General Erich von Falkenhayn, Chief of the General Staff, orders the start of experiments with chemical weapons.

The uniformed Haber goes off to the front lines at Ypres, puffing his cigar, and calculates the timing of a lethal gas attack. Thousands of steel chlorine-gas cylinders are in readiness at the German positions. After weeks of waiting for ideal prevailing winds in Belgium to float the gas away from their own troops, the Germans, supervised by Haber in person, release more than 168 tons of chlorine gas from nearly 6,000 canisters. The sickening yellow cloud asphyxiates 5,000 French and Belgian soldiers. Haber is triumphant.

'What drives people to kill and maim each other so savagely?' Albert asks Heinrich Zangger. 'I think it is the sexual character of the male that leads to such wild explosions.'

CLARA HABER

Back in Berlin, Haber arranges a grand party to celebrate his success marked by promotion to the rank of captain.

His pacifist wife, Clara, aged forty-four, had graduated *magna cum laude* from the University of Breslau and gained her doctorate in chemistry, the first woman to receive a PhD in Germany. A newspaper reported Clara's recitation of the oath: 'never in speech or writing to teach anything that is contrary to my beliefs. To pursue truth and to advance the dignity of science to the heights which it deserves.' She is revolted by her husband's work. She's already protested about it in public. She declares it to be a 'perversion of the ideals of science. A sign of barbarity, corrupting the very discipline which ought to bring new insights into life.' Her husband's delight and pride in chemical warfare is repugnant. She pleads with him to cease working on gas warfare. He tells her and anyone who'll listen that she's making statements treasonous to the Fatherland.

In a letter to her friend and mentor Richard Abegg, who taught her as a *Privatdozent* (outside lecturer) at Wrocław University of Science and Technology, she complains that Fritz's gain has been her loss.

After the party, during the early hours, Clara takes her husband's service pistol out into the garden and shoots herself.

Her thirteen-year-old son, Hermann, hears the shot and alerts his father. Clara dies in Hermann's arms.

Next morning, leaving Hermann to deal with matters, Haber goes to the Eastern Front to organise the first gas attack on the Russians. Clara's suicide remains secret until six days afterwards, when the local newspaper, *Grunewald-Zeitung*, reports that 'the wife of Dr Haber in Dahlem, who is currently on the front, has set an end to her life by shooting herself. The reasons for this act of the unhappy woman are unknown.'

*

Albert follows the Second Battle of Ypres in the newspaper. After the artillery bombardment of the enemy's line, the Allied defenders wait for the first wave of German attack troops. Haber's chlorine gas wafts across no man's land into their trenches, slaughtering two divisions of French and Algerian colonial troops.

The savagery of Haber's perverted science is unbounded.

During the last few months of the war, the Americans come to the Western Front. Austria-Hungary, Germany's closest ally, begins to fall apart. Czechoslovakia, Poland and Hungary seek independence.

The Kaiser finds himself facing General Ludendorff advising that he sue for peace. Prince Maximilian Alexander Friedrich Wilhelm, Margrave of Baden, forms a cabinet. The Bund Neues Vaterland pacifists demand political prisoners be released.

Germany is losing the battle in France and the German navy mutinies.

The Kaiser goes into exile in the Netherlands on 9 November 1918.

Two days later, Germany signs the armistice prepared by Britain and France and the guns fall silent.

The Great War ends at 11 a.m. on the eleventh day of the eleventh month.

The war between Albert and Mileva drags on. Both sides blame sickness. Mileva says she doesn't want to block his route to happiness. She tells Albert to have his lawyer write to hers. Exasperated, Albert finally agrees to make a deposition in Berlin for the Zürich divorce court admitting to his adultery.

Early the following year he gives a series of lectures in Switzerland and on Valentine's Day, a month before Albert's birthday, the divorce is finalised. However, in the immediate aftermath of the war to end all wars, a state of familial turmoil follows the settlement matching Germany's political chaos. Mileva and her offspring require expensive medical treatment in sanatoria and hospitals as well as nursing at home.

Tete falls victim to the epidemic of influenza not once but twice.

'What can you do?' Elsa asks him.

'About the children? I am always the organ player who can do nothing more than turn and turn . . . do you want to hear my little poem?'

Elsa smiles.

> I am as I always am the organ player
> Who can do nothing more than turn and turn
> Until the sparrow sings it from the roof
> And the last scoundrel comprehends it.

The last scoundrel fails to keep a secret of his passion for another woman. No less than Ilse, the twenty-one-year-old second daughter of his bride-to-be.

Ilse tells Georg Nicolai: 'Yesterday, the question was suddenly raised about whether A. wishes to marry Mama or me . . . Albert is refusing to take any decision; he is prepared to marry me or Mama. I know that A. loves me very much, perhaps more than any other man ever will, he also told me so himself yesterday . . . I have never wished or felt the least desire to be close to him physically. This is otherwise in his case – recently at least. – He himself even admitted to me how difficult it is for him to keep in check . . .'

Albert then invites Ilse to become his secretary.

'Why?' she says.

'Reason: preservation and possibly enhancement of your maidenly charms. I'm about to travel to Norway. I will take either Elsa or you, Ilse. You are more suitable because you are healthier and more practical.'

ANOTHER POSTCARD FROM ELSA

'Come to bed, Albertli,' Elsa says, undressing.

'Will you wear your special nightie, Mama?'

She puts on the nightdress.

Albert raises it above her waist and she holds him tight and guides him inside her.

When gratified he rolls away from her, sighing, 'I love you, Ilse. Ilse . . . My love.'

Elsa tenses. 'What did you call me?'

'My love.'

'You called me Ilse. You make love to me and you call me by my daughter's name.'

'What are you saying?'

'So that's it. You are obsessed with Ilse.'

'It was a slip of the tongue.'

'Your tongue has been in my mouth. Your penis has been inside my cunt. Do you do that to Ilse?'

'No. I do not.'

'Do you love her?'

'No. I do not.'

'No more Ilse,' Elsa says. 'No more.'

'No more Ilse,' says Albert. 'No more Ilse.'

'Do you want me to be your wife?'

'You know that's what I want – more than anything in the world.'

'How will you prove it, Albertli?'

'With an equation.'

'With an equation? I don't want an equation. I want you.'

'Good. Then $A + E = E + A$. That's my gift to you.'

'I have a gift for you, Albertli.'

'What is it?'

'I will make sure you become world-famous.'

122

'Men marry women with the hope they will never change. Women marry men with the hope they will change.

Invariably they are both disappointed.'

Albert Einstein

ELSA AND ALBERT, 2 JUNE 1919

The responsibility for the elevation of Albert to the status of worldwide celebrity isn't Elsa's. The international press generates it.

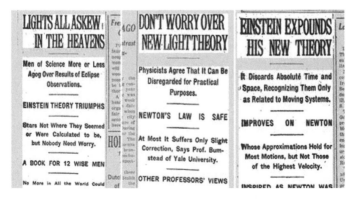

THE NEW YORK TIMES, **10 NOVEMBER, 16 NOVEMBER AND 3 DECEMBER 1919**

A NEW EMINENCE IN THE HISTORY OF THE WORLD: ALBERT EINSTEIN, WHOSE RESEARCHES SIGNIFY A COMPLETE REVOLUTION OF OUR UNDERSTANDING OF NATURE AND WHOSE INSIGHTS EQUAL IN IMPORTANCE THOSE OF A COPERNICUS, KEPLER, AND NEWTON

Two years later, in 1921, to mark Albert's first visit to the United States, William Carlos Williams writes 'St Francis Einstein of the Daffodils':

> . . . April Einstein
> through the blossomy waters
> rebellious, laughing
> under liberty's dead arm

has come among the daffodils
shouting
that flowers and men
were created
relatively equal.
Old-fashioned knowledge is
dead under the blossoming peach trees . . .

PAULINE EINSTEIN IN HER LAST DAYS

On a visit to her daughter, Maja, and son-in-law, Paul, in Lucerne, Pauline, now aged sixty-two, is diagnosed with terminal stomach cancer and admitted to the Rosenau Sanatorium.

Albert brings her to Haberlandstrasse 5, where he and Elsa care for her. During her last days he tries to raise her spirits by reciting the news of his successes.

After her death, Albert tells Elsa: 'Now I know what it's like to

125

see one's mother go through the agony of death and be unable to help; there is no consolation. We all have to bear such heavy burdens, for they are unalterably linked to life.'

Albert tells Paul Ehrenfest he's disillusioned with politics.

'During the war I thought the Allied victory would be far the lesser evil. Now I think they seem to be only the lesser evil.'

'What d'you mean?' Ehrenfest asks.

'There's the thoroughly dishonourable domestic politics: the reactionaries with all their shameful deeds in repulsive revolutionary disguise. One doesn't know where to look to take pleasure in human striving.'

'Do you really get no pleasure from the way things are going?'

'What makes me happiest is the realisation of a Jewish state in Palestine. Our brethren really are nicer, at least less brutal, than these awful Europeans. Maybe it can only get better if the Chinese alone survive; they lump all Europeans together as "bandits".'

KURT BLUMENFELD

126

Kurt Blumenfeld, a German-born Zionist from Marggrabowa in East Prussia and secretary-general of the World Zionist Organisation, visits Albert in Berlin. Blumenfeld sounds him out about Zionism.

'I'm against nationalism but in favour of Zionism,' Albert tells him. 'When a man has both arms and he is always saying I have a right arm, then he is a chauvinist. However, when the right arm is missing, then he must do something to make up for the missing limb.'

'You oppose Zionism?'

'No. As a human being, I'm an opponent of nationalism. But as a Jew I'm a supporter of the Jewish Zionist efforts. The Zionist cause is very close to my heart. I'm very confident of the happy development of the Jewish colony and am glad that there should be a tiny speck on this earth in which the members of our tribe should not be aliens. One can be internationally minded, without renouncing interest in one's tribal comrades. I will give my support to Chaim Weizmann. I've received numerous invitations to lecture in America. Weizmann proposes I accompany him and make appearances in the East Coast cities. Additionally, I am to deliver lectures at Princeton. I will consider Weizmann's notion carefully.'

Albert is mindful that the tour in America will earn him some money in a stable currency to provide for Mileva in Switzerland. 'I've asked $15,000 from Princeton and Wisconsin,' he tells Ehrenfest. 'It will probably scare them off. But if they do bite, I'll be buying economic independence for myself – and that's not a thing to sniff at.'

The American universities won't pay up. 'My demands were too high.' he tells Ehrenfest.

So he makes plans to present a paper at the third Solvay Conference in Brussels and lecture for Ehrenfest in Leiden.

Yet when Albert is asked to address the Centralverein, the Organisation of Germans of the Jewish Faith, he tells them that 'efforts of assimilationist Jews to put aside everything Jewish appear somewhat comical to a non-Jew, because the Jews are a people apart. The psychological root of anti-Semitism lies in the fact that the Jews are a group of people unto themselves. Their Jewishness is visible in their physical appearance, and one notices their Jewish heritage in their intellectual work.'

Then Chaim Weizmann delivers Albert a telegram from the World Zionist Organisation inviting Albert and Elsa to America on a tour to raise funds for a university in Jerusalem.

Albert accepts: 'I am not at all eager to go to America but am doing it only in the interests of the Zionists, who must beg for dollars to build educational institutions in Jerusalem and for whom I act as high priest and decoy . . . I do what I can to help those in my tribe who are treated so badly everywhere.'

It's in the bag.

He tells Friedrich Zangger: 'On Saturday I'm off to America – not to speak at universities, though there will probably be that, too, on the side, but rather to help in the founding of the Jewish University in Jerusalem. I feel an intense need to do something for this cause.'

Elsa is thrilled. 'You may serve as my interest when necessary,' Albert tells her.

'I will tell the Americans all about my Albert,' she says.

'Perfect,' says Albert. 'Perfect.'

CHAIM WEIZMANN

One person who's enraged by Albert's decision is Fritz Haber, who's converted from Judaism to appear a fully-fledged Prussian. Haber reckons that a visit by Albert to the wartime enemy on behalf of a Zionist organisation will emphasise the idea that Jews are bad Germans.

Haber had been delighted that Albert would attend the Solvay Conference in Brussels. 'People in this country will see this as evidence of the disloyalty of the Jews,' Haber writes when he hears of Albert's decision to visit America.

Albert takes issue with Haber's way of seeing Jews as being people of the Jewish faith. 'Despite my emphatic internationalist beliefs,' Albert says, 'I have always felt an obligation to stand up for my persecuted and morally oppressed tribal companions. The prospect of establishing a

Jewish university fills me with particular joy, having recently seen count-less instances of perfidious and uncharitable treatment of splendid young Jews with attempts to deny their chances of education.'

**ALBERT AND ELSA SET SAIL FROM HOLLAND,
CROSSING THE ATLANTIC ABOARD THE SS *ROTTERDAM*,
A JOURNEY OF NINE DAYS**

NEW YORK CITY

On arrival at the Port of New York, the mayor John Hylan presents Albert and Weizmann with the Freedom of the City.

During a procession from Battery Park to the Hotel Commodore, thousands of Zionists carrying the blue-and-white striped flag of Zion, with the Star of David in the centre, line the streets to catch a glimpse of their leaders. Albert receives a tumultuous greeting. Mayor Hylan's welcome committee calls upon the guests at the hotel to escort them to City Hall. As Albert leaves the building he is lifted to the shoulders of his colleagues in the automobile, which passes in triumphal procession through the mass.

The mayor greets the party in the reception room of the City Hall. Albert wanders about in a pair of worn-out trousers and a sweater with a distant, bewildered expression, causing members of the delegation to nudge him now and then into shaking the hands of his devoted admirers. Because so many want to hear the speeches, they're delivered on the steps.

The press can't get enough of him.

The *City News* representative asks: 'Will you be good enough to tell us in one sentence exactly what your theory of relativity is?'

'All my life,' Albert says in German, 'I have been striving to get it into one book. And you want me to state it in one sentence.'

The man from the *Tribune* asks: 'Professor, what do you think of America?'

'Excuse me, I have not yet arrived in America.'

'What do you think of American women?'

'Excuse me, I haven't yet met with American women.'

'Professor, how will your theory benefit the man in the street,' asks *The New York Times* man.

Albert looks around in dismay and leaves the room in a melee, followed by Elsa who's lost a gold lorgnette. The mayor offers a reward for its recovery. To no avail.

There's an official Zionist reception at the packed Metropolitan Opera House on Broadway and 39th Street.

The audience roars its approval when the visitors appear on stage. 'Hatikvah' is sung.

> Our hope is not yet lost,
> The hope two thousand years old
> To be a free nation in our land,
> The land of Zion and Jerusalem.

Albert addresses a rally of thousands at the 69th Regiment Armory on Lexington Avenue. President Harding wires greetings: 'This visit must remind people of the great service that the Jewish race has rendered humanity.'

Marion Weinstein of the *American Hebrew* interviews Elsa. Elsa reads out selected passages for Albert's benefit. "She has the beauty of a fine painting. She is the type men love for their innate womanliness, artists choose for their 'Madonnas' and Jews picture as the ideal 'mother of Israel'. Mrs Einstein was wearing a simple cloth skirt and a purple silk, daintily embroidered overblouse. You associate her with deep, refreshing pools and balmy sunshine. Her fine blue eyes and pretty teeth flash with laughter, as she tells you some of her *amusing* experiences in this maelstrom of America."

'You couldn't have written it better yourself,' Albert says.

'Neither could you,' says Elsa.

They head to Washington DC, where Albert gives a talk to the National Academy of Sciences.

President Harding is unenthusiastic about meeting Albert and Elsa at the White House but receives them anyway, saying he doesn't understand relativity.

Albert gives five lectures on relativity at Princeton, where he receives an honorary doctorate.

Then on to Harvard and Boston with Weizmann. In Boston a brass band greets him. In the evening Mayor Andrew J. Peters hosts a kosher banquet. The mayor says: 'Not many of us can follow Professor Einstein in his discussion of the mathematical properties of space; but all of us can understand his refusal to sign that manifesto condoning the invasion of Belgium.'

On to Cleveland, where Jewish merchants close up shop and pour onto the streets to cheer him.

Albert tells Besso: 'Two frightfully exhausting months now lie behind me, but I have the great satisfaction of having been very useful to the cause of Zionism and of having assured the foundation of the university . . . It's a wonder I was able to hold out. But now it's over, and there remains the beautiful feeling of having done something truly good.'

Exhausted, Albert and Elsa return to Europe aboard the British White Star Line's RMS *Celtic*, a journey of some nine days.

On 24 June 1922, Albert's friend, the foreign minister of the Weimar Republic, Walther Rathenau, leaves his house in Grunewald, ten minutes from Berlin, in his open car. At the junction of Wallotstraße and Königsallee a car draws up alongside Rathenau's and blocks it. A gunman fires five shots, another man throws a hand grenade into the car. Rathenau dies instantaneously.

Rathenau had often told Albert that he served a Germany that didn't like him. 'My heart is heavy . . . what can a man like that do in this paralysed world with enemies all around?' Rathenau had received numerous death threats. He heard the members of the Upper Silesian Selbstschutz, a quasi-military organisation, chanting: 'God damn Walther Rathenau. Shoot him down, the dirty Jew.' The police advised him to carry a handgun.

Rathenau's assassins are a law student, Erwin Kern, twenty-three, and a mechanical engineer, Hermann Fischer, twenty-six, both of them blond and blue-eyed former army officers and members of the right-wing anti-Semitic terrorist group, Consul. Ernst Werner Techow is at the wheel.

The killers flee to Saaleck Castle in Naumberg, some 200 kilometres south of the German capital. But they make the mistake of leaving a light on, and local residents, aware that the tenant, a far-right sympathiser, is absent, alert the police. The police try to arrest Kern, who yells: 'Long live Ehrhardt.' The police shoot him dead. Fischer shoots himself. Techow is arrested and sentenced to fifteen years in jail. The state prosecutor cites 'blind hatred of Jews' as the motive.

German nationalists carry out the murders of several hundred government officials and radical activists. Two radical German nationalists unsuccessfully attempt to assassinate Philipp Scheidemann, former Social Democratic Chancellor of the Weimar Republic, by spraying hydrogen cyanide in his face.

On the day of Rathenau's funeral, Heidelberg's Nobel Prize-winning professor of physics, Philipp Lenard, forbids students to skip his lecture 'because of a dead Jew'. Lenard refuses to lower the flag as a mark of respect and is dragged from his laboratory by a furious mob of students who try to chuck him into the River Neckar. The university reprimands him and he resigns. When he finds out that the shortlist for his replacement is made up of two non-Aryans, James Franck and Gustav Hertz, he withdraws his resignation.

To Albert these academic-political manoeuvres are chaff blowing in the air compared to the political rumours shaking Germany to the core.

His life has been nerve-racking since the assassination of Rathenau. He's constantly on the alert. He's stopped his lectures and is officially absent. Anti-Semitism is virulent.

Weizmann paints a dark picture: 'All the shady characters of the world are at work against us. Rich servile Jews, dark fanatic Jewish obscurantists, in combination with the Vatican, with Arab assassins. English imperialist anti-Semitic reactionaries – in short, all the dogs are howling. Never in my life have I felt so alone – and yet so certain and confident.'

Albert and Elsa agree. They should take themselves away from the remorseless tide of hate.

'Read this,' Albert tells Elsa. 'The words of the devil spoken in Munich's *Hofbräuhaus*.'

The Jew has not grown poorer: he gradually gets bloated, and, if you don't believe me, I would ask you to go to one of our health-resorts; there you will find two sorts of visitors: the German who goes there, perhaps for the first time for a long while, to breathe a little fresh air and to recover his health, and the Jew who goes there to lose his fat. And if you go out to our mountains, who do you find there in fine brand-new yellow boots with splendid rucksacks in which there is generally nothing that would really be of any use? And why are they there?

They go up to the hotel, usually no further than the train can take them: where the train stops, they stop too. And then they sit about somewhere within a mile of the hotel, like blowflies round a corpse.

These are not, you may be sure, our working classes: neither those working with the mind, nor with the body. With their worn clothes they leave the hotel on one side and go on climbing: they would not feel comfortable coming into this perfumed atmosphere in suits which date from 1913 or 1914. No, assuredly the Jew has suffered no privations! And the Right has further completely forgotten that democracy is fundamentally not German: it is Jewish. It has completely forgotten that this Jewish democracy

135

with its majority decisions has always been without exception only a means towards the destruction of any existing Aryan leadership. The Right does not understand that directly every small question of profit or loss is regularly put before so-called 'public opinion', he who knows how most skilfully to make this 'public opinion' serve his own interests becomes forthwith master in the State. And that can be achieved by the man who can lie most artfully, most infamously; and in the last resort he is not the German, he is, in Schopenhauer's words, 'the great master in the art of lying' – the Jew.

In boundless love as a Christian and as a man I read through the passage which tells us how the Lord at last rose in His might and seized the scourge to drive out of the Temple the brood of vipers and of adders. How terrific was His fight for the world against the Jewish poison.

Today, after two thousand years, with deepest emotion I recognise more profoundly than ever before – the fact that it was for this that He had to shed His blood upon the Cross. As a Christian I have no duty to allow myself to be cheated, but I have the duty to be a fighter for truth and justice. And as a man I have the duty to see to it that human society does not suffer the same catastrophic collapse as did the civilisation of the ancient world some two thousand years ago – a civilisation which was driven to its ruin through this same Jewish people.

'The words of Satan,' Elsa says.

Albert always cheered up at the mention of Bertrand Russell's name. He read me a copy of a letter Russell sent to Lady Colette Malleson. 'What a queer work the Bible is . . . Some texts are very funny. Deut. XXIV, 5: "When a man hath taken a new wife, he shall not go out to war, neither shall he be charged with any business: but he shall be free at home one year, and shall cheer up his wife which he hath taken." I should never have guessed "cheer up" was a Biblical expression. Here is another really inspiring text: "Cursed be he that lieth with his mother-in-law. And all the people shall say, Amen." St Paul on marriage: "I say therefore to the unmarried and widows, It is good for them if they abide even as I. But if they cannot contain, let them marry: for it is better to marry than to burn." This has remained the doctrine of the Church to this day. It is clear that the Divine purpose in the text "it is better to marry than to burn" is to make us all feel how very dreadful the torments of Hell must be.'

Mimi Beaufort, Princeton, New Jersey

The Japanese publisher and writer Sanehiko Yamamoto asks Russell to suggest the names of the world's two greatest thinkers to lecture in Japan. Russell offers Lenin and Einstein.

Lenin is too preoccupied with the governance of the Russian Soviet Federative Socialist Republic to accept. The prospect of a long voyage by sea appeals to Albert; so does the pay. And he can take Elsa along too. But then he receives quite another invitation. Rather, a hint of an invitation.

This one is from the director of the Nobel Institute of Physical Chemistry in Stockholm, Svante Arrhenius. Awarded the Nobel Prize in Chemistry in 1905, he also has a keen interest in physics. Arrhenius has got wind of the invitation to Japan. He writes to Albert: 'It will probably be very desirable for you to come to Stockholm in December. If you are then in Japan that will be impossible.'

Albert is in two minds about the invitations.

It's twelve years since he was first nominated by Ostwald for his work on special relativity. The Swedish committee prevaricated because it was felt the prize should be given to 'the most important discovery or invention'. The committee needed more evidence before awarding Albert the prize. From then on Albert was regularly nominated: by Wilhelm Wien, physics laureate himself in 1911, co-editor of *Annalen der Physik*, and successor to Röntgen as Professor of Physics at the University of Munich. Niels Bohr supported him. So did Lorentz. On the other hand, Lenard was heading the crusade against Albert, the protagonist of 'Jewish science'. It was the Swiss Charles Édouard Guillaume, head of the International Bureau of Weights and Measures in Sèvres, who won the prize in 1920.

The following year Albert received fourteen nominations, including Planck's and Arthur Eddington's. There remained formidable opposition, most conspicuously from Allvar Gullstrand at the University of Uppsala, where he was professor of ophthalmology and Nobel laureate in Physiology in 1911.

Gullstrand dismissed Albert's work. But he mistakenly said that the effects of general relativity 'measurable by physical means are, however, so small that, in general they lie below the limits of experimental error'. He also offered misinterpretations of experiments by others.

Arrhenius's report on the photoelectric effect was equally dismissive. The result was that the decision on the recipient of the Nobel Prize in Physics for 1921 was delayed till the next year, when Albert was once more proposed. Gullstrand was commissioned to bring his report on relativity up to date. Once again he came out against Albert. Another member of the committee, Carl Wilhelm Oseen, Director of the Nobel Institute for Theoretical Physics in Stockholm, was asked to re-evaluate the photoelectric effect and found in Albert's favour. Albert would be awarded the deferred 1921 prize – but not for relativity. He would be given it for his 1905 explanation of the photoelectric effect, in which electrons are emitted from a metal sheet only under certain illuminations. Thus the prize would be awarded to Albert for a law not a theory.

The committee's ploy was to give both Albert and Niels Bohr a prize: Albert's seemingly backdated to 1921, Bohr's contemporaneously in 1922.

Arrhenius carefully kept the tangled machinations of the committee to himself.

Albert reflects that, in 1915, he promised that if he one day received the Nobel Prize the money will be given to Mileva. This will amount to 135,000 Swedish kronor. She'd initially dismissed the idea, then changed her mind.

The question is: north to Scandinavia or east to the Orient?

The Orient wins out.

'How long will we be away for?' Elsa asks.

'Six months. Maybe longer.'

In October 1922, Albert and Elsa leave Berlin squashed into the overnight train for Marseilles, where they board the Japanese postal vessel SS *Kitano Maru*. The journey to Kobe will take over a month.

Albert and Elsa sit on deck watching their Japanese fellow passengers, particularly the playful children. 'Those little faces,' Albert enthuses, 'remind me of flowers. *Sakura* – Japanese cherry. *Momo* – peach. *Sakurasou* – primula. So pretty. So pretty.'

He reads Henri Bergson's *Durée et simultanéité à propos de la théorie d'Einstein*. Albert is not convinced by Bergson's notion that experience and intuition are more significant than abstract rationalism and science for understanding reality and turns instead to his copy of Ernst Kretschmer's *Body Structure and Character*, in which Kretschmer argues that physical properties of the face, skull and body are related to character and psychiatric illness.

Albert explains to Elsa that Kretschmer 'diligently measures and

139

photographs patients and considers his research as both psychiatry and anthropology'.

In the privacy of their cabin between the engine rooms and hull they strip naked and compare and contrast each other.

Three main body types:

A. Asthenic (thin, small, weak): associated with introversion and timidity, resembling a milder form of the negative symptoms of schizophrenics
B. Athletic (muscular, large-boned): epileptic.
C. Pyknic (stocky, fat): friendly, interpersonally dependent and gregarious, are predisposed towards manic-depressive illness.

Albert says, 'We are C.'

'I am G,' says Elsa.

'What's G?'

'Gemütlichkeit.'

'Ah!'

'Come to bed,' says Elsa. 'I'll prove it.'

The SS *Kitano Maru* stops briefly at Port Said, steams south through the Red Sea and the Gulf of Aden and across the Arabian Sea.

Off the coast of Sumatra, Albert is thrilled to see a Fata Morgana mirage, his excitement only diminished by painful haemorrhoids and violent diarrhoea.

Fortunately, Professor Hayari Miyake, a specialist in surgery of the gastrointestinal tract and central nervous system, is a fellow passenger. He recommends Albert drinks eight glasses of water and walks thirty minutes a day on deck to stimulate his bowel movements.

Unfortunately, fellow passengers bombard him for requests to be photographed and he has to start and end his walks before dawn.

Arriving in Singapore, Albert finds Chaim Weizmann has contacted the Jewish community in advance and Albert succeeds in getting a £500 donation for the Hebrew University from the tycoon and philanthropist Sir Manasseh Meyer.

Albert sketches a written portrait of Meyer in his diary: 'Croesus is still a slender, upright eighty-year-old man with a strong will. A small grey pointed beard, a thick reddish face, a narrow Jewish bent nose, clever, somewhat shrewd eyes, a small black cap, a well-arched forehead. Resembling Lorentz, yet the shining benevolent eyes of the latter are replaced by guarded sly ones, and the facial statement reflects more schematic order and work, rather than love for mankind and solidarity as in Lorentz's case.'

After a stop in Hong Kong, the *Kitano Maru* steams up the Yangtze, arriving at Shanghai on 13 November 1922. A choir sings 'Deutschland Über Alles' by way of welcome. Then the official party comes aboard. The German consul, Pfister, and his wife. The physicist Inagaki and his wife. Finally, the Swedish consul-general, Christian Bergstrom, introduces himself and hands Albert two envelopes.

The first is postmarked 'Stockholm 10.11.1922'.

Albert opens it and reads a telegram: 'Awarded Nobel Prize in Physics. More details follow soon. C. Aurivillius.'

The second is similarly postmarked 'Stockholm den 10 November 1922'. Albert reads:

As I have already informed you by telegram, the Swedish Academy of Sciences decided at yesterday's meeting that you are awarded for 1922 the Nobel Prize for Physics as a reward for your work in theoretical physics and especially for your discovery of the law of the photoelectric effect, but without regard of your relativity

– and theories of gravitation. Following notice of acceptance, on 10 December, the awards of diplomas and gold medals to the prize winners will be confirmed at the Annual General Meeting.

On behalf of the Academy of Sciences, I invite you therefore to attend to witness the prize and receive it personally.

If you come to Stockholm, it would be best if you deliver your lecture the day following the prize-giving.

In the hope that the Academy will have the joy of seeing you here in Stockholm. With consideration respectfully yours

Chr. Aurivillius
Secretary

'Well?' says Elsa.

'It is interesting news. Interesting news.'

'What interesting news?'

'The Swedish consul-general says congratulations.'

'Congratulations on what? Why d'you look so happy?'

'A table, a chair, a bowl of fruit and a violin; what else does a man need to be happy?'

Elsa reads the telegram and the letter and bursts into tears.

That night Albert and Elsa dine at the Yin Pin Xiang restaurant accompanied by dignitaries from the worlds of education and a posse of awed Japanese journalists.

Albert is seated next to Liu-Wang Liming. The German consul tells him Liu-Wang is the publisher of *Women's Voice*, a bi-weekly magazine, and a pioneer of women's writings on politics.

She is sensitive to Albert's mood.

'You seem', she says, 'almost indifferent to the award of your Nobel Prize.'

'Do you know *Macbeth*?'

'Of course.'

'"Out, out, brief candle! Life's but a walking shadow, a poor player, that struts and frets his hour upon the stage, and then is heard no more. It is a tale told by an idiot, full of sound and fury, signifying nothing."'

'The idea that "all the world's a stage" is depressing?'

'Precisely. "Whoever undertakes to set himself up as a judge in the field of Truth and Knowledge is shipwrecked by the laughter of the gods." I've kept my good humour and take neither myself nor the next person seriously. Remember Mark Twain: "The gods offer no rewards for intellect. There was never one yet that showed any interest in it."'

'What will you say at the ceremony?'

'I would like to say something like "if we want to resist the powers which threaten to suppress intellectual and individual freedom we must keep clearly before us what is at stake, and what we owe to that freedom which our ancestors have won for us after hard struggles".'

'Which powers d'you have in mind?'

'The Nationalsozialistische Deutsche Arbeiterpartei. The Nazi Party.'

The stay in Shanghai is brief. Albert and Elsa are relieved to be back aboard the *Kitano Maru*, which steams across the Yellow Sea and a week later docks in Kobe.

From Kobe they head to Kyoto, stay overnight at the Miyako Hotel, then travel on to Tokyo, a rail journey of ten hours.

The German ambassador to Japan, Wilhelm Heinrich Solf, reports back to Berlin:

Professor Einstein's journey through Japan resembles a triumphal procession. The entire population, from the highest dignitary to the rickshaw coolie, is taking part, spontaneously, without any preparation or fuss. At Einstein's arrival in Tokyo, such a huge throng was waiting at the station that the police were powerless to control the life-endangering crowds. Thousands upon thousands of Japanese throng to his lectures – at 3 yen per head – and Einstein's scholarly words are translated into yens that flow into Mr Yamamoto's pockets.

Two thousand people pack the largest lecture hall at Keio University to hear him talk about relativity. His first lecture is scrupulously translated sentence by sentence by Professor Yun Ishiwara. It lasts four hours.

There are tea ceremonies, lunches, dinners, a chrysanthemum festival, receptions, visits to Buddhist temples, concerts. 'All eyes were on Einstein,' says the German ambassador. Albert lectures in Sendai, northeast of Tokyo on Honshu island; in Nikko, in the mountains to the north of Tokyo; in Nagoya, in the Chūbu region; in Kyoto, and in Fukuoka on the northern shore of Japan's Kyushu island. In the port of Moji he plays his violin for children at the YMCA Christmas Day party.

Next day Albert and Elsa leave Japan aboard the SS *Haruna Maru*, which heads west across the Indian Ocean.

The journey by steamship and finally by ferry to Lod, southeast of Tel Aviv, lasts almost two months. Albert feels happy and at ease. He loves the stars in the clear night skies. By day, he completes his comments on Eddington's relativity ideas in time to post it to Planck from Port Said.

The captain marks the last night at sea by hosting a farewell banquet, during which a British widow gives Albert a pound for the University of Jerusalem.

PALESTINE, 1922

Sir Herbert Samuel, first British high commissioner of Palestine, is Albert and Elsa's host.

Albert is entranced by the Jordan valley, the Bedouins, Jericho's ancient ruins, and the severity of the landscape, which he calls 'magnificent'.

The attorney general, Norman Bentwich, and his wife, Helen, arrange a musical evening in Albert's honour. Albert plays Mozart on a borrowed violin.

Tel Aviv makes him an honorary citizen. He tells the audience: 'I have already had the privilege of receiving honorary citizenship of the City of New York, but I am tenfold happier to be a citizen of this beautiful Jewish town.'

He gives the first lecture at the, as yet, unconstructed Hebrew

University, and visits Haifa, where he plants two palm trees in the Technion, the school of engineering and sciences.

Wherever he goes people want to shake his hand and congratulate him on his Nobel Prize.

Albert is delighted.

The final leg of the journey aboard SS *Oranje* is to Toulon. From Toulon they take a train to Marseilles and on to Barcelona.

Albert gives three packed lectures at the Institut d'Estudis Catalans. The Einsteins are chaperoned by the German consul, Christian August Ulrich von Hassell, and his wife, Ilse von Tirpitz, daughter of Grand Admiral Alfred von Tirpitz.

In Madrid, he speaks at the Academy of Sciences during a session hosted by King Alfonso XIII. Albert and Elsa go to Toledo with the philosopher Ortega y Gasset. Albert is deeply moved by El Greco's *The Burial of Count Orgaz* in the Church of Santo Tomé. He visits the Prado, marvelling at the paintings by Fra Angelico, Raphael, Goya, El Greco and Velázquez.

In the middle of March they return to Berlin.

They find it costs 10 million marks to buy a loaf of bread; a kilogram of beef, 76 million marks.

NOBEL LECTURE, GOTHENBURG, 11 JULY 1923

The Jubileum Hall in Gothenburg's Liseberg amusement park provides the unlikely setting for Albert's Nobel lecture on a July day of blistering heat. Intended to be a marvel of new architecture, a jewel marking the three-hundredth anniversary of Gothenburg's founding, the hall is walled almost entirely in glass. More than 900 people have come to hear him. Numerous members of the audience complain that they are sticking to their newly lacquered seats. The lecture will last an hour. The perspiring King Gustav sits at the front in a grand chair in the central aisle.

The audience falls silent.

'I will speak on the theory of relativity,' says Albert. 'The title: Fundamental Ideas and Problems of the Theory of Relativity.'

Albertli has such a sweet speaking voice. He's speaking to me. No matter that I've heard it all before and have never understood a word of it.

It's so hot in here. I am perspiring. My armpits are soaked.

Fortunately the men beside Elsa are listening to Albert in rapt attention so she can rummage unnoticed in her handbag for her phials of aromatic perfumes: Aventure, with its notes of cedar wood, amber and pink pepper, Linde Berlin, which evokes Berlin's famously fragrant linden trees, and Violet, based on a perfume created for Marlene Dietrich.

Albert is in full flight. 'The special theory of relativity is an adaptation of physical principles to Maxwell-Lorentz electrodynamics. From earlier physics it takes the assumption that Euclidian geometry is valid for the laws governing the position of rigid bodies, the inertial frame and the law of inertia.'

She dabs a copious amount of scent on a silk handkerchief and applies it to her face.

You'd think someone could open a window.

A man behind her begins to cough. Obviously an inveterate smoker, he hawks up phlegm. Elsa can hear him wheezing.

Albert ignores the coughing. 'The special relativity theory

147

resulted in appreciable advances. It reconciled mechanics and electro-dynamics. It reduced the number of logically independent hypotheses regarding the latter.'

Elsa slips a Luden's cough drop beneath her tongue.

She wonders whether there's anyone else in the audience who hasn't a clue what Albertli's saying. The more incomprehensible he becomes the more she assumes a look of intense concentration. Not that Albertli will be fooled. But, ah, the others in the audience will be.

Incredible, they'll think . . . incredible Mrs Einstein under-stands. A brilliant woman.

'It enforced the need for a clarification of the fundamental concepts in epistemological terms. It united the momentum and energy principle, and demonstrated the like nature of mass and energy.'

After about half an hour, the combination of the heat and lack of fresh air brings on drowsiness.

Elsa's eyelids get heavier. Her head drops forward and she sits up straight with a jerk.

'Should the form of the general equations some day, by the solution of the quantum problem, undergo a change however profound, even if there is a complete change in the parameters by means of which we represent the elementary process . . .'

Almost there. Elsa sits up straight.

'. . . the relativity principle will not be relinquished and the laws previously derived therefrom will at least retain their significance as limiting laws.'

That's it.

He receives tumultuous applause. Elsa is euphoric.

The cheering goes on and on.

Albert smiles and bows.

Elsa looks at him in adoration. Her Albert looks so much younger than his forty-four years.

ALBERT WITH MORITZ KATZENSTEIN

On his return to Berlin, the future of Germany depresses him.

He confides in a friend he first encountered during the war, Moritz Katzenstein, director of the department of surgery at the Berlin Municipal Hospital in Friedrichshain. In 1900 Katzenstein successfully sewed together a six-year-old girl's torn meniscus. It was the first time the operation had been performed in Germany.

Albert, whose heart has been troubling him, appreciates Katzenstein's consultations and the pair sail together.

Albert and Elsa regularly entertain Katzenstein, and Albert values the hours spent on Katzenstein's yacht on the Wannsee.

'I am told,' Albert says to Katzenstein, 'that the Reich Commissioner for the Surveillance of Public Order has me under surveillance as a member of the German League of Human Rights. I am a political alien and an enemy of the state.'

'Are you going to leave, Albert?'

'Privately – it's on my mind. Look at the facts. The Nazis claim that nearly ten thousand of their thugs have been wounded in clashes with their opponents. The Communists report seventy-five in the first six months of this year alone. Think of Hermann Göring's Bremen rally. Blackjacks, brass knuckles, clubs, heavy buckled belts, glasses and bottles were employed. Chair legs used as bludgeons. Blood everywhere. Göring stood on the stage, his fists on his hips. Grinning.'

He pauses to admire a passing Abeking & Rasmussen Windfall sloop. One of the crew has binoculars focused on Albert, alerts two girls on deck, who wave and shout: '*Hooray for Professor Einstein!*'

Albert waves back.

The girls blow him kisses.

Tears begin to stream down Albert's cheeks.

'Sometimes one pays most for the things one gets for nothing,' he says.

'You've done great things for Germany,' Katzenstein says.

'I've only enhanced Germany's prestige and never allowed myself to be alienated by the systematic attacks on me in the rightist press, especially those of recent years when no one took the trouble to stand up for me. Now, however, the war against my defenceless Jews compels me to employ, on their behalf, whatever influence I may possess in the eyes of the world.'

'It hasn't come to that, Albert.'

'It will, Moritz, you see.' His voice is quavering. 'It will.'

The London *Times* asks Albert to write an article about his discoveries and he readily agrees.

His tone disguises his anguish.

Sir,

I gladly accede to the request of your colleague to write something for *The Times* on relativity. After the lamentable breakdown of the old active intercourse between men of learning, I welcome this opportunity of expressing my feelings of joy and gratitude toward the astronomers and physicists of England. It is thoroughly in keeping with the great and proud traditions of scientific work in your country that eminent scientists should have spent much time and trouble, and your scientific institutions have spared no expense, to test the implications of a theory which was perfected and published during the war in the land of your enemies.

Some of the statements in your paper concerning my life and person owe their origin to the lively imagination of the writer. Here is yet another application of the principle of relativity for the delectation of the reader: today I am described in Germany as a 'German savant', and in England as a 'Swiss Jew'. Should it ever be my fate to be represented as a bête noire, I should, on the contrary, become a 'Swiss Jew' for the Germans and a 'German savant' for the English.

Sincerely yours,

Albert Einstein

As his fame increases so too does the antagonism of his rivals in Berlin. The antagonism is inflamed by praise from other quarters. Arthur Eddington, leader of the 1919 British solar-eclipse expedition to the island of Principe off the western coast of Africa, confirms Albert's prediction, founded upon his general theory of relativity, that the gravitational field of the Sun will bend light. Eddington calls Albert the Newton of his time.

The public acclaim borders on adulation. Albert and Elsa bask in it. Here he is, a Jew, a democrat, a pacifist: a figure unacceptable to the Weimar Republic's reactionary elements, which gear up to assault him. The anti-Semite Paul Weyland begins the denunciation and intended destruction of Albert's reputation.

It starts with a provocative article by Weyland in the *Tägliche Rundschau*, a Berlin daily newspaper. 'Herr Albertus Magnus has been resurrected. He has stolen the work of others and has mathematised physics to such an extent that fellow physicists have been left clueless. Relativity is propaganda, a fraud and fantasy.' Weyland publishes another article in the right-wing *Deutsche Zeitung* against the German National People's Party position on the 'Jewish question': too gentle for his liking, so he says. He dismisses the account of the British eclipse expedition in *Die Naturwissenschaften*. He derides the comparisons with Copernicus, Kepler and Newton in the *Berliner Tageblatt* and *Berliner Illustrirte Zeitung*. Albert himself is to blame for it.

He follows up his attack in front of 1,600 people in the Berlin Philharmonic Hall's large auditorium.

'Hardly ever in science has a scientific system been set up with such a display of propaganda as the general principle of relativity, which on closer inspection turns out to be in the greatest need of proof.'

DIE BERLINER PHILHARMONIKER HALLE

Anti-Semitic pamphlets are handed out, and swastika lapel pins are available for purchase.

Albert is at the lecture. He sits next to Elsa, who holds his hand. Profoundly upset, Elsa listens with tears in her eyes.

With his other hand Albert drums out a melody on his knee: Mozart's Twelve Variations on 'Ah, vous dirai-je, Maman', K.265, 'Twinkle, Twinkle, Little Star'.

They stay on for Ernst Gehrcke's lecture.

According to Gehrcke, 'relativity is scientific mass hypnosis; inconsistent, solipsistic, and unconfirmed by observation.'

Twinkle, twinkle, little star.

Albert and Elsa have no doubt that the attacks are founded upon anti-Semitism. The new Weimar Republic is simmering with suppressed violence and rage.

Albert is infuriated by the rumours that he will leave Germany.

Letters of support flood in from Jews, pastors, professors and students.

Writing from Leiden, Paul Ehrenfest tells Albert that if he elects to leave Germany, arrangements can be made to find a professorship for him in the Netherlands.

The Berlin newspapers print letters in his support from von Laue, Heinrich Rubens and Walther Nernst. Max Planck and Fritz Haber beg him not to leave Berlin. Albert confronts it head-on with a statement in the mass circulation *Berliner Tageblatt*.

Albert judges that the anti-relativity company has pretty much broken down and jokingly observes that he's not going to 'flee the flag', as Sommerfeld put it. 'My opponents had the splendid idea to engage my dear friends for their business. You can imagine how I had to laugh when I read this . . . ! I came to see the funny side of this whole affair a long time ago and no longer take any of it seriously.'

To Elsa, Albert admits he's been wounded.

SOCIETY OF GERMAN SCIENTISTS AND PHYSICISTS
IN BAD NAUHEIM, 1920

'Why does Lenard hate us?' Elsa asks.

'Because he's an anti-Semite. Bottled up. Stunted. Self-important. He is a run-of-the-mill scientist.'

'With a Nobel Prize.'

'Which guarantees nothing. I embody all he loathes. And the English congratulate me. To Lenard I am a Jewish fraud. Because I am a Jew I am a fraud. That's his theory. He's not alone in holding it. He maintains all disputes in physics are the responsibility of Jews. He believes that everything has a spiritual essence. As in the *Naturphilosophie* of Goethe and Schelling. Only Aryans understand that it's the yearning of Nordic man to investigate a hypothetical interconnectedness in nature which is the origin of natural science.'

Elsa nods sagely.

'Materialism infects Communism and the Jewish spirit, the enemies of German grandeur. It's mysticism and pseudo-science.'

'You are right, Albert.'

'He is a mediocrity.'

'He hates you – because you are a great spirit.'

'Great spirits have always found violent opposition from mediocrities.'

*

In the spa town of Bad Nauheim, Bathhouse No. 8, the audience of 600 gather at 8.15 p.m. The entry system is complex. A single narrow door is held open. Officials of the Union of German Mathematicians and the German Physical Society vet those attending. At 9 p.m. everyone's allowed in. The audience grab chairs, others stand along the walls and fill the gallery.

First, Hermann Weyl lectures, then Gustav Mie, Max von Laue and Leonhard Grebe, until finally proceedings open for a general debate of fifteen minutes.

Hecklers interrupt Albert. The chairman, Planck, has difficulty keeping order. The debate is confused and inaudible.

Elsa is greatly distressed.

After the proceedings have ended, the Austrian physicist Felix Ehrenhaft and his wife take Albert and Elsa for a restorative walk in the park, then for dinner away from fellow physicists.

Albert says to Elsa and the Ehrenhafts: '"Blood and destruction shall be so in use, / And dreadful objects so familiar, / That mothers shall but smile when they behold / Their infants quarter'd with the hands of war." The violence is increasing. Anti-Semites "cry 'Havoc!' and let slip the dogs of war".'

*

Again he and Elsa go abroad. This time to Argentina, Brazil and Uruguay.

They leave Hamburg aboard the liner *Cap Polonio*. Albert enjoys the company of the philosopher Carl Jesinghaus and takes a shine to the feminist Else Jerusalem, author of the bestselling *Red House,* a study of prostitution in Vienna. He gives her a photograph of himself inscribed:

> This is for the Panther Cat,
> Even though she went to hide
> In the jungle harsh and wild.
> This picture's for her
> In spite of that.

In Buenos Aires, Montevideo and Rio de Janeiro, Albert and Elsa meet with an endless procession of government officials, academics, and Jewish and German dignitaries.

5TH SOLVAY CONFERENCE, OCTOBER 1927

In October 1927, Albert joins the world's most distinguished physicists for the 5th Solvay Conference, staying at the Hotel Britannique in Brussels. Seventeen of the twenty-nine present are or will become Nobel laureates.

Albert, Lorentz and Max Planck are sceptical about the present state of quantum physics. Albert, now forty-eight, faces much younger opponents like Louis de Broglie, Paul Dirac, Werner Heisenberg and Wolfgang Pauli, as well as his old friend and rival, Niels Bohr.

Bohr offers the view that there's no point talking of reality.

Albert says little during the proceedings. Preferring to discuss the issues informally, he says: 'One can't make a theory out of a lot of "maybes". Deep down it's wrong, even if it's empirically and logically right.'

He's disenchanted with Heisenberg's uncertainty principle. He says: 'God does not play dice with the universe.'

Bohr counters: 'Einstein, stop telling God what to do.'

Albert is battling for the scientific realists, who seek strict rules for scientific methods, against Bohr and the instrumentalists, who want flexible rules based on outcomes. They maintain the truth of an idea is determined by its success in the active solution of a problem, and the value of an idea is determined by its function in human experience.

'I believe,' Bohr tells Planck, 'that the restriction to statistical laws will be a passing one.'

For the time being it's an impasse.

To make matters worse, Albert hears that Lorentz has died in Holland.

He attends the funeral in Haarlem and the memorial service at the University of Leiden:

It is as the representative of the German-speaking academic world, and in particular the Prussian Academy of Sciences, but above all as a pupil and affectionate admirer that I stand at the grave of the greatest and noblest man of our times. His genius was the torch, which lighted the way from the teachings of Clerk Maxwell to the achievements of contemporary physics, to the fabric of which he contributed valuable materials and methods.

His life was ordered like a work of art down to the smallest detail. His never-failing kindness and magnanimity and his sense of justice, coupled with an intuitive understanding of people and things, made him a leader in any sphere he entered. Everyone followed him gladly, for they felt that he never set out to dominate but always simply to be of use. His work and his example will live on as an inspiration and guide to future generations.

HELEN

It is Elsa's idea that Helen Dukas takes on the role of Albert's secretary. She's thirty-two; Albert's forty-nine. Elsa is friends with Rosa Dukas, Helen's sister, who runs the Jewish Orphans Organisation. Elsa is an honorary president.

Albert receives Helen at Haberlandstrasse 5. Albert immediately likes her.

In August 1930, he opens the 7th German Radio Show in Berlin: 'Think gratefully of the number of unknown engineers who simplified the instruments of communication via radio and its production in such a fashion that they are ready to be used by everybody. And everybody should be ashamed who uses the wonders of science and engineering without thinking, having understood no more of it than a cow understands the botany of the plants it eats with pleasure.'

The whirligig of travel spins on.

Albert again sets off, this time from Antwerp for America, on the SS *Belgenland* with Elsa and Helen Dukas, along with the mathematician Walther Mayer.

Telegrams pour in during the turbulent transatlantic voyage, begging for interviews and lectures in the United States.

In New York City, they chat with Toscanini and watch him conduct Beethoven's *Pastoral.*

The President of Columbia University, Nicholas Butler, calls Albert the 'visiting monarch of the mind'.

AT THE GRAND CANYON

HOPI INDIANS

160

CHARLIE CHAPLIN

In Los Angeles they meet Charlie Chaplin, who invites them to dinner with Paulette Goddard, William Randolph Hearst and Marion Davies, and then to be his special guests at the premiere of *City Lights*.

'What I admire most about your art is its universality,' Albert tells Chaplin. 'You do not say a word, and yet the world understands you.'

'It's true,' says Chaplin. 'But your fame is even greater. The world admires you when nobody understands you.'

Outside the Los Angeles Theater, thousands yell and shout beneath searchlights sweeping across the sky.

'What does all this mean?' Albert asks Chaplin.

'Nothing,' says Chaplin. 'Nothing.'

Will Rogers, actor, comedian and newspaper columnist, records: 'The radios, the banquet tables and the weeklies will never be the same. He came here for a rest and seclusion. He ate with everybody, talked with everybody, posed for everybody that had any film left, attended every luncheon, every dinner, every movie opening, every marriage and two-thirds of the divorces. In fact, he made himself such a good fellow that nobody had the nerve to ask what his theory was.'

Albert writes in his diary: 'Today I decided, in principle, to give up my position in Berlin. And so I'll be a migratory bird for the rest of my life!'

HUNDERT
AUTOREN GEGEN EINSTEIN

Herausgegeben
von
Dr. HANS ISRAEL, Dr. ERICH RUCKHABER,
Dr. RUDOLF WEINMANN

Mit Beiträgen von
Prof. Dr. DEL-NEGRO, Prof. Dr. DRIESCH, Prof. Dr. DE HARTOG,
Prof. Dr. KRAUS, Prof. Dr. LEROUX, Prof. Dr. LINKE, Prof. Dr.
LOTHIGIUS, Prof. Dr. MELLIN, Dr. PETRASCHEK, Dr. RAUSCHEN-
BERGER, Dr. REUTERDAHL, Dr. VOGTHERR u. v. a.

1931
R. VOIGTLÄNDERs VERLAG · LEIPZIG

'A HUNDRED AUTHORS AGAINST EINSTEIN'

Back in Berlin, Albert corresponds with Freud. 'Is there any way of delivering mankind from the scourge of war?' Albert asks.

Freud replies:

How long have we to wait before the rest of men turn pacifist? Impossible to say, and yet perhaps our hope that these two factors – man's cultural disposition and a well-founded dread of the form that future wars will take – may serve to put an end to war in the near future, is not chimerical. But by what ways or byways this will come about, we cannot guess. Meanwhile we may rest on the assurance that whatever makes for cultural development is working also against war.

With kindest regards and, should this exposé prove a disappointment to you, my sincere regrets,

Yours,
Sigmund Freud

The political atmosphere causes him the greatest agitation. He gains temporary respite by going to Oxford to lecture, only to find that the formality of the senior common room in Christ Church stifles him.

Abraham Flexner, founder of the Institute for Advanced Study in Princeton, visits him at Christ Church. They walk together around the smooth lawns of Tom Quad. Flexner proposes that Albert come to Princeton on any terms he wishes. Albert says he'll consider Flexner's generous proposal.

Perhaps, he wonders, there'll be a reversal in the march of Hitler and the Nazis. This year. Next year. Some time.

CAPUTH

He struggles to keep his life in order, to create a sense of permanence.

So he builds a brand new house, mainly of Oregon pine and Galician fir, in Caputh, a quiet and dreamy village in the municipality of Schwielowsee, Potsdam-Mittelmark, Brandenburg.

He and Elsa divide their time between Haberlandstrasse 5 and Caputh with their housekeeper, Herta Schiefelbein. Helen Dukas and Walther Mayer join them. Albert even begins to think of living there permanently. The quiet, with no telephone, holds a greater appeal than the interminable meetings of the Prussian Academy of Sciences. He plays with his dog, Purzel. Max Born visits them, along with Ehrenfest, the artist Käthe Kollwitz, writer Arnold Zweig, Sommerfeld, Weizmann, and Rabindranath Tagore.

Albert steps up the tempo and force of his public speeches.

To the Marxist Workers' School he lectures on 'What the Worker Needs to Know About the Theory of Relativity'. He says: 'I respect Lenin as a man who did everything in his power to achieve social justice, at great cost to himself. I do not consider his method suitable. But one thing is certain: men like Lenin are the guardians and restorers of the conscience of mankind.'

Finally Flexner visits Caputh. They talk all day and over dinner, until Albert accompanies Flexner to the bus stop and sees him on to the Berlin bus. Albert explains that if he and Elsa were to go to America he wants Mayer to go too. The deal is almost done.

In December 1932, before departing for Pasadena, he writes to his old friend Maurice Solovine, asking for copies of his works to be sent from Paris to Caputh.

Albert receives a decisive message from a member of parliament, General Johannes Friedrich von Seeckt, known as the Sphinx. Albert doesn't know who's told the general to get in touch. Von Seeckt tells him, 'Your life is not safe here any more.'

To Elsa, Albert says: 'Look around. You won't see it again.'

With no fewer than thirty pieces of luggage they board the SS *Oakland* at Bremerhaven for California. They face an uncertain future.

PASADENA

GARDENS OF THE ATHENAEUM

In Pasadena the climate is in every sense the opposite. Albert strolls in the gardens of the Athenaeum, the private social club of the California Institute of Technology. He talks with Evelyn Seeley of the *New York World Telegram.* 'As long as I have any choice in the matter, I shall live only in a country where civil liberty, tolerance and equality of all citizens before the law prevail.'

EARTHQUAKE, LOS ANGELES, 10 MARCH 1933

Shortly after Seeley leaves, an earthquake strikes Los Angeles, killing 116 people. Albert scarcely notices. Walking across campus, Albert feels the ground shaking under his feet and does a little dance.

On 30 January 1933, Hitler becomes Chancellor. Nazis gather outside the Haberlandstrasse apartment and his office at the Academy of Science, screaming abuse and decrying 'Jewish science'. Their hatred is concentrated against Albert.

In Caputh, a baker complains to his customers about Albert's 'Jewish house'.

The Third Reich bars Jews and Communists from the universities. None are allowed to practise law or work in the civil service.

The Nazis raid the Caputh house, loot the wine cellar, smear the walls with excrement, and scatter furniture and linen sheets around the garden.

In Berlin, they raid and ransack the Haberlandstrasse apartment. Margot is terrified. She manages to get news to her husband, Dimitri Marianoff, who tells her to take Albert's papers to the French ambassador, François-Poncet – who's made repeated warnings about Hitler's intentions – then leave as soon as possible for Paris. Margot immediately does so. Ilse and her husband, Rudolf Kayser, succeed in getting to Amsterdam.

For Albert, the time has come to return to Europe, though not Berlin.

En route, he arrives in Chicago – on his fifty-fourth birthday – to attend a Youth Peace Council rally. Speakers vow that the pacifist cause must continue despite what's happening in Germany. Some leave with the impression that Albert is in full agreement.

At a birthday luncheon that day, he speaks of the need for international organisations to keep the peace. No mention of war resistance.

Again, at a New York reception for an anthology of his writings on pacifism, *The Fight Against War*, he refers only in passing to events in Germany.

Just before Albert's due to sail for Antwerp, Paul Schwartz, German consul in New York, warns him not to set foot in Germany. 'If you do, they'll drag you through the streets by the hair.'

After the Institute for Advanced Study opens the following year, he plans to visit Princeton for four or five months annually. The day before they set sail, he and Elsa visit Princeton to look for a house.

Aboard the SS *Belgenland*, with Elsa, Helen Dukas and Walther Mayer, Albert is heartbroken to learn that the Nazis have raided his Haberlandstrasse apartment and the house in Caputh, and, into the bargain, have confiscated their sailing boat, *Tümmler*.

Albert tells Elsa and Helen: 'The universities that pride them-

167

selves upon their intellectual freedom have failed me. I look to the German press, which prides itself on the freedom of the press, and it fails me. Now only the churches stand alone, and that for which I once had little regard earns my respect.'

He writes a letter to the Prussian Academy submitting his resignation: 'Dependence on the Prussian government is something that, under the present circumstances, I feel to be intolerable.'

After ten days the *Belgenland* docks in Antwerp.

He has a car drive him the forty-five kilometres to the German consulate in Brussels. There he surrenders his passport and, for the second time in his life, renounces his German citizenship. It's the only way that ensures an honourable severance of his relations with the Academy.

Alarmed by the violence of the anti-Semitic diatribes against Albert in the Nazi press, Planck is meanwhile trying to get round the formal disciplinary hearings the government seeks. 'Starting formal exclusion procedures against Einstein would bring me into gravest conflicts of conscience,' he writes to the Academy secretary. 'Even though on political matters a deep gulf divides me from him, I am, on the other hand, absolutely certain that in the history of centuries to come, Einstein's name will be celebrated as one of the brightest stars that ever shone in the Academy.'

The Nazis are enraged that Albert has outmanoeuvred them by publically renouncing both his citizenship and Academy membership. So a Nazi secretary of the Academy issues a press release. This denounces Albert's 'participation in atrocity-mongering and his activities as an agitator in foreign countries. The Academy has, therefore, no reason to regret Einstein's withdrawal.'

Albert fires back: 'I hereby declare that I have never taken any part in atrocity-mongering. I described the present state of affairs in Germany as a state of psychic distemper in the masses.'

True.

Lenard fumes: 'The most important example of the dangerous influence of Jewish circles on the study of nature has been provided by Herr Einstein.'

The government passes a law declaring that Jews cannot hold any official position, with the result that fourteen Nobel laureates and twenty-six professors of theoretical physics flee Germany.

Hitler rages: 'If the dismissal of Jewish scientists means the annihilation of contemporary German science, then we shall do without science for a few years.'

'For me,' Albert says, 'the most beautiful thing is to be in contact with a few fine Jews – a few millennia of a civilised past do mean something after all.'

Close to 40,000 students and beer-hall drunks sporting swastikas chuck books onto the bonfire in front of Berlin's opera house. The books have been looted from private homes and libraries.

VILLA SAVOYARDE, LE COQ-SUR-MER

Albert, Elsa, Helen and Walther Mayer stay at the Villa Savoyarde in Le Coq-sur-Mer, ten kilometres from Ostend.

From here, he writes to Maurice Solovine: 'My great fear is that this hate and power epidemic will spread throughout the world. It comes from below to the surface like a flood, until the upper regions are isolated, terrified and demoralised, and then also submerged.'

'We can all go to Zürich,' Albert says over a late breakfast. 'The family will be united.'

'I don't think so,' says Elsa. 'You will be psychologically worn out by the strain.'

'We can't go to Leiden or Oxford.'

The maître d' hurries to their table, wringing his hands, with an officer of the Ostend gendarmerie.

The officer comes straight to the point. 'Professor, I am sorry to have to tell you there's now a five thousand dollar bounty on your head.'

'Really?' says Albert. 'My head? I didn't know it was worth that much.'

'From now on there will be two armed officers protecting you.'

'I don't want that.'

'You have no alternative.'

ALBERT AND HIS BELOVED TETE

Michele Besso, Albert's close friend during his years at the ETH in Zürich, tells Albert that his son Tete's schizophrenia has worsened. He's now permanently in an asylum.

Albert goes to Zürich to see Mileva and Tete. He takes his violin to play to Tete. Locked into another world, Tete stares at Albert blankly.

Albert tries to comfort Mileva. 'Unfortunately, as I recently told Besso, everything indicates that strong heredity manifests itself very definitely. I have seen that coming slowly but inexorably since Tete's youth. Outside influences play only a small part in such cases, compared to internal secretions, about which nobody can do anything.'

'Nothing?'

'Nothing.'

They embrace in silent grief.

Albert leaves Zürich. It is the last time he will see Mileva and Tete.

He has received an invitation to visit England. He hopes it will offer him a respite from his emotional exhaustion.

WITH OLIVER LOCKER-LAMPSON AND BODYGUARD

Oliver Locker-Lampson is the adventurous son of the Victorian poet Frederick Locker-Lampson. He had been a student in Germany, a World War I aviator, led an armoured division in Lapland and Russia, was an adviser to Grand Duke Nicholas, and a potential participant in the murder of Rasputin. Now a barrister, journalist and MP, he is an early opponent of Nazism. He writes to Albert offering to be his host in England.

Together they motor down to Chartwell to see Winston Churchill.

WITH WINSTON CHURCHILL

Germany's rearmament is the topic of conversation. Albert tells Churchill about the fate of Jewish scientists in Germany. Churchill says he'll ask his friend Frederick Lindemann to see what can be done to place them in British universities. 'Churchill's an eminently wise man,' Albert tells Elsa. 'It became clear to me that these people have made preparations and are determined to act resolutely and soon.'

Locker-Lampson introduces Albert to Austen Chamberlain, another rearmament advocate; and to Lloyd George, former prime minister. Albert signs the visitors' book. As his address he writes '*Ohne irgendetwas*': 'without anywhere'.

Next day Locker-Lampson speaks in the House of Commons about extending opportunities of citizenship for Jews. Albert, in his white linen suit, watches on from the visitors' gallery. 'Germany is in the process of destroying its culture and threatening the safety of its greatest thinkers. She has turned out her most glorious citizen, Albert Einstein.'

The bill Locker-Lampson proposes never sees the light of day.

AT THE ROYAL ALBERT HALL

Albert's most keenly anticipated appearance is arranged by the Academic Assistance Council at the packed Royal Albert Hall, to raise money for displaced German academics. Albert speaks in his heavily accented English.

I am glad that you have given me the opportunity of expressing to you here my deep sense of gratitude as a man, as a good

European, and as a Jew. It cannot be my task today to act as a judge of the conduct of a nation which for many years has considered me as her own. We are concerned not merely with the technical problem of securing and maintaining peace, but also with the important task of education and enlightenment.

If we want to resist the powers which threaten to suppress intellectual and individual freedom we must keep clearly before us what is at stake, and what we owe to that freedom which our ancestors have won for us after hard struggles. Without such freedom there would have been no Shakespeare, no Goethe, no Newton, no Faraday, no Pasteur and no Lister. There would be no comfortable houses for the mass of people, no railway, no wireless, no protection against epidemics, no cheap books, no culture and no enjoyment of art at all. There would be no machines to relieve the people from the arduous labour needed for the production of the essential necessities of life.

Most people would lead a dull life of slavery, just as under the ancient despotisms of Asia. It is only men who are free, who create the inventions and intellectual works which to us moderns make life worthwhile.

*

Back at Le Coq-sur-Mer, Albert learns that the American anti-suffrage newspaper *Woman Patriot Corporation* seeks to bar him as a dangerous Communist subversive. His record as a pacifist and anti-fascist suggests Albert's sympathetic to Russian Communism.

'I am a convinced democrat,' he tells the *New York World Telegram*. 'It is for this reason that I do not go to Russia, although I have received very cordial invitations. My voyage to Moscow would certainly be exploited by the rulers of the Soviets to profit their own political aims. Now I am an adversary of Bolshevism just as much as of fascism. I am against all dictatorships.'

To *The Times* of London and *The New York Times,* Albert admits that sometimes he's been 'fooled' by organisations that pretend to be pacifist or humanitarian but 'are in truth nothing less than camouflaged propaganda in the service of Russian despotism. I have never favoured Communism and do not favour it now. I oppose any power that enslaves the individual by terror and force, whether it arises under a Fascist or Communist flag.'

He receives a letter from Paul Ehrenfest in Leiden: 'In recent years it has become ever more difficult for me to follow the developments in physics with understanding. After trying, ever more enervated and torn, I have finally given up in desperation. I am completely weary of life.'

Albert writes to the board of the University of Leiden, expressing deep concern and suggesting ways in which Ehrenfest's workload can be reduced. Ehrenfest, now fifty-three, has always been harder on himself than anyone else. He exaggerates his shortcomings and inadequacies. His chronic melancholy is worse than ever. To complicate his state of mind further, he can no longer face the fact that his beloved son Wassik has Down syndrome and requires lifelong clinical care, a heavy financial burden.

On 25 September 1933 Paul Ehrenfest travels with a handgun from Leiden to a laboratory in Amsterdam to visit a former student of his. In the afternoon Ehrenfest leaves the laboratory and goes to the Vossiusstraat, where he collects Wassik, now fifteen, from the clinic where he's institutionalised. Father and son go to the Vondelpark, west of Leidseplein and the Museumplein. There Ehrenfest shoots Wassik in his head and then himself.

Albert had treated him like a brother, was like an uncle to his children. He is devastated.

In his grief Albert recalls his first meeting with Paul Ehrenfest. 'Within a few hours we were true friends – as though our dreams and aspirations were meant for each other.'

SS *WESTERNLAND*

The 16,500-ton Red Star Line's SS *Westernland* sails from Antwerp with Elsa and Helen Dukas aboard.

An unmarked police car deposits Albert on the Southampton quayside, where he's taken by launch to board the ship for New York.

Albert stands alone on deck. He struggles to light his pipe against the Atlantic spray.

He's grieving for Ehrenfest.

For his own past.

Southampton disappears in the October mist.

A tie has been cut. The die cast.

The gulls sweep above the ship's wake. Ship horns blare out in melancholy chorus.

He will never see Europe again.
Or the religious paradise of youth.
Albert is fifty-four years old.

►►►►◄ FOUR ►►►►◄

I discovered that one of the first things Albert did on arrival in Princeton was to buy an ice cream cone at the Baltimore ice cream parlor on Nassau Street. He ordered vanilla with chocolate sprinkles. A divinity student, John Lampe, watched Albert. 'The great man looked at the cone, smiled at me . . . and pointed his thumb first at the cone and then at himself.'

A group of girl trick-or-treaters knocked on his door on Halloween night. Albert stepped out on to the front porch and played his violin for them.

Mimi Beaufort, Princeton, 1955

In October 1933, Albert and Elsa, along with Helen Dukas, check in to the Peacock Inn in Princeton. Elsa searches for a suitable house and Albert avoids reporters.

After a week they move to temporary accommodation on the corner of Mercer and Library streets.

THE HAPPY COUPLE

Albert soon becomes a subject of curiosity in Princeton.

Safe and sound, he loves the peaceful milieu. He greets dogs and children. Pauses to admire trees and flowers: American hollies, oaks, hydrangeas, ashes and Princeton elms, calculating when the oaks and ashes will come into leaf. 'When the oak is before the ash, then you will only get a splash; when the ash is before the oak, then you may expect a soak.'

Harvard awards him an honorary doctorate.

The president of Harvard, J.B. Conant, says of Albert: 'Acclaimed by the world as a great revolutionist of theoretical physics, his bold speculations, now become basis doctrine, will be remembered when mankind's present troubles are long forgotten.'

Albert hasn't for a moment forgotten Europe. He tells a reporter from Vienna's *Bunte Welt*, 'I cannot understand the passive response of the whole civilised world to this modern barbarism. Doesn't the world see that Hitler is aiming for war?'

Walter Kreiser, a writer for *Die Weltbühne*, exposes the secret training of an elite air unit of the Reichswehr Abteilung M (M Battalion) in Germany and Soviet Russia, in violation of the Treaty of Versailles. Kreiser and Carl von Ossietzky, the paper's editor, are indicted for treason and espionage and sentenced to eighteen months in jail. Kreiser flees Germany but Ossietzky stays, is imprisoned and released after a few months during the Christmas amnesty.

Ossietzky is rearrested and held in Spandau. Then at the Papenburg-Esterwegen concentration camp near Oldenburg, second largest concentration camp after Dachau.

Albert contacts Jane Addams, the pioneering social worker, feminist and Nobel laureate, and suggests she propose Ossietzky for the 1935 peace prize. When she does so, he writes: 'Dear Mrs Jane Addams! Thank you so much for supporting Ossietzky, who unfortunately won't be able to endure the brutal treatment much longer. People here cannot imagine the cruelty suffered by all progressive people who are being persecuted in Germany.'

A substantial number of scientists and politicians join the campaign worldwide.

An International Red Cross inspector finds Ossietzky 'a trembling, deadly pale something, a creature that appeared to be without feeling, one eye swollen, teeth knocked out, dragging a broken, badly healed leg . . . a human being who had reached the uttermost limits of what could be borne.' He's also suffering from tuberculosis.

When Ossietzky is awarded the Nobel Peace Prize, Göring orders him to decline it. Ossietzky replies from the hospital:

After much consideration, I have made the decision to accept the Nobel Peace Prize which has fallen to me. I cannot share the view put forward to me by the representatives of the Secret State Police that in doing so I exclude myself from German society. The Nobel Peace Prize is not a sign of an internal political struggle, but of understanding between peoples. As a recipient of the prize, I will do my best to encourage this understanding and as a German I will always bear in mind Germany's justifiable interests in Europe.

Two members of the prize committee – Halvdan Koht, Norway's foreign minister, and Sigmund Mowinckel – resign. King Haakon VII stays away from the ceremony. The Norwegian newspaper *Aftenposten* says: 'Ossietzky is a criminal who's attacked his country with the use of methods that violated the law long before Hitler came into power. Lasting peace between peoples and nations can only be achieved by respecting the existing laws.'

No mention of Ossietzky's Nobel Prize is permitted in the German press and the government forbids German citizens from accepting Nobel prizes.

Ossietzky dies three years later, aged forty-eight, still in police custody in the Nordend hospital in Berlin-Pankow, from tuberculosis and the after-effects of the abuse he suffered at the hands of his guards.

The move to Princeton and the setting up of their home in Mercer Street exhausts Elsa. She learns of the death of Ilse from tuberculosis in Paris.

She falls ill and doctors diagnose myocarditic exophthalmic goitre and lobar pneumonia. She coughs up blood.

Albert confides in Helen Dukas: 'I can't bear to see her in so much pain.'

'She knows how much you love her.'

'D'you think so?'

'Yes. She told me that your concern for her is a great comfort.'

In the summer they take a holiday on Saranac Lake in the Adirondack Mountains.

The doctor administers morphine.

Elsa tries to knit a scarf. Her legs and ankles swell up. Her heart and kidneys weaken.

Aged sixty, five days before Christmas 1936, Elsa dies at home in Princeton.

Grief immobilises Albert.

A funeral service is held at the Mercer Street house. Then Elsa is cremated at the Ewing Cemetery at 78 Scotch Road.

Albert collapses in Helen's arms.

'Think of the future,' she says.

'I shall really miss her – I shall really miss her.'

THE CREATURE OF ROUTINE

Albert follows a strict routine. Breakfast at 9 a.m. Eggs fried in butter, and a teaspoonful of honey. Fresh bread rolls.

He walks to the Institute, frequently waylaid by locals who want to meet the great man. He poses for photographs, signs autographs, and offers a few jovial words.

He works at the Institute till 1 p.m.

Returns home for lunch, usually spaghetti. Takes a short siesta.

Works in his study until 6.30 p.m. and dinner. Returns to his study and works until 11 p.m.

Bed.

DR. EINSTEIN SIMPLIFIES A FORMULA.

EINSTEIN 'REPAIRS' MASS-ENERGY IDEA

'THE PRESS WON'T LEAVE ME ALONE'

The New York Times declares:

> Soaring over a hitherto unscaled mathematical mountain-top, Dr Albert Einstein, climber of cosmic Alps, reports having sighted a new pattern in the structure of space and matter. Einstein revealed today that after twenty years of unremitting search for a law that would explain the mechanism of the cosmos in its entirety, reaching out from the stars and galaxies in the vastness of infinite space down to the mysteries within the heart of the infinitesimal atom, he has at last arrived within sight of what he hopes may be the 'Promised Land of Knowledge', holding what may be the master key to the riddle of creation.

*

His search to unify everything is a lonely one. He writes to von Laue: 'I feel like a kid who cannot get the hang of the ABCs, even though, strangely enough, I do not abandon hope. After all, one is dealing here with a sphinx, not with a willing streetwalker.'

He writes to Solovine: 'I am working with my young people on an extremely interesting theory with which I hope to defeat the modern proponents of mysticism and probability and their aversion to the notion of reality in the domain of physics.'

During the months before the outbreak of war in 1939, there's a frantic pursuit of new ideas in physics.

In Berlin, at the Kaiser-Wilhelm Institute, Otto Hahn and Fritz Strassmann find that atomic nuclei can be split. This nuclear fission can release a vast amount of energy relative to atomic mass. The notion is of course contained in $E = mc^2$. A chain reaction could produce a gigantic amount of energy.

185

Within a few months no fewer than twenty articles on nuclear fission appear in *Nature*.

WITH LEO SZILARD

Son of an engineer and scion of an affluent Jewish family, Leo Szilard was born Leo Spitz in Budapest, changing his name to Szilard in 1900. In Berlin, he studied engineering at the Institute of Technology and was attracted to the work of physicists such as Albert, Haber, Nernst, Planck, von Laue and Schrödinger. In 1921 Szilard gave up his engineering studies and enrolled at the University of Berlin, where he studied physics under Max von Laue, among others. He gained his doctorate with a dissertation demonstrating that the Second Law of Thermodynamics covers not only the mean values, as was up to then believed, but also the fluctuating values. Between 1925 and 1933, he applied for numerous patents, often with Albert, including one for a new refrigeration system in which they tried and failed to interest AEG.

After Hitler's rise to power Szilard moved to England, where he collaborated with T.A. Chalmers at St Bartholomew's Hospital and developed the Szilard–Chalmers process to chemically separate radioactive elements from their stable isotopes. At the same time, he influenced Sir William Beveridge to found the Academic Assistance

Council to help persecuted scientists leave Nazi Germany. Between 1935 and 1937 he worked as a research physicist at Oxford's Clarendon Laboratory.

In September 1933, Szilard conceived of the possibility of a nuclear chain reaction – the process essential for the releasing of atomic energy – something that Lord Rutherford, Britain's pre-eminent physicist, had recently dismissed.

Like Albert, Szilard visits America several times in the 1930s, considers moving there, and finally settles in New York City in 1938.

In the Pupin Laboratories at Columbia University, Szilard collaborates with Walter Zinn on neutron emissions. They work out that two fast neutrons are emitted in the fission process, and that uranium might sustain a chain reaction. More research with Enrico Fermi and Herbert Anderson at Columbia shows that water and uranium oxide meet the requirements for a self-sustaining chain reaction.

Szilard is seriously concerned about the applications of the new atomic theories to the development of weapons. German nuclear research is at an advanced stage, and he feels that the work being conducted by him and his colleagues should be withheld from publication. Szilard and two further colleagues, Eugene Wigner and Edward Teller, want the US government to underwrite a definitive experiment to prove a sustained nuclear chain reaction is possible.

This is why Leo Szilard and Eugene Wigner seek out Albert. They want Albert to write a letter to President Roosevelt. A letter with Albert's imprimatur will carry enormous weight with the State Department.

And set in motion the development of a weapon of colossal power. X-ray-heated air will form a gigantic fireball that will send out shock waves at a velocity greater than the speed of sound and cause loss of life and destruction on an unimaginable scale.

*

187

Albert is staying at a rented cottage on Old Grove Road, Peconic, Long Island. Szilard and Wigner explain the plan. The letter is drafted and redrafted.

It takes two months of blundering around to find a conduit to get the letter signed by Albert into the hands of the person who could take decisive action: President Roosevelt. The conduit is the Jewish-American banker, Alexander Sachs.

On 11 October 1939, Sachs goes to the White House to see Roosevelt.

Sachs tells Albert about the meeting. FDR is distant and tells him the idea is premature.

Sachs won't give up. He returns to the White House next morning.

Roosevelt is sitting alone at his breakfast table.

'All I want to do is to tell you a story, Mr President. During the Napoleonic wars a young American inventor came to the French Emperor and offered to build a fleet of steamships with the help of which Napoleon could, in spite of the uncertain weather, land in England. Ships without sails? This seemed to the great Corsican so impossible that he sent Robert Fulton away. In the opinion of the English historian Lord Acton, this is an example of how England was saved by the shortsightedness of an adversary. Had Napoleon shown more imagination and humility at that time, the history of the nineteenth century would have taken a very different course.'

The President examines his favourite *Berliner Pfannkuchen* – hot, jam-filled doughnuts – in silence.

He scribbles a note and hands it to a servant.

'Wait,' he tells Sachs.

The servant returns carrying a package containing a bottle of vintage French brandy. The President tells the servant to fill two glasses. Then he raises his, nods to Sachs and drinks to him.

'Alex, what you are after is to see that the Nazis don't blow us up?'

'Precisely.'

Roosevelt calls in his attaché, Brigadier General Edwin 'Pa' Watson. He points to Sachs' letter.

'Pa, this requires action.'

J. Edgar Hoover, director of the Federal Bureau of Investigation for sixteen years, alleges that Albert is an extreme radical, has written for Communist magazines. Hoover opposes Albert's employment on any secret naval or military matter.

Albert, Helen and Margot decide to become American citizens. They pass the test before a federal judge in Trenton, New Jersey.

Albert, Helen and Margot follow an unwavering routine in Princeton, learning of the progress of the war in the newspapers and on radio.

The New York Times.

FIRST ATOMIC BOMB DROPPED ON JAPAN; MISSILE IS EQUAL TO 20,000 TONS OF TNT; TRUMAN WARNS FOE OF A 'RAIN OF RUIN'

Helen Dukas gives Albert the news of Hiroshima at the cottage in the Adirondacks.

'Oh, my God.'

Three days later the second bomb strikes Nagasaki.

Next day Washington issues a report outlining the influence Albert's letter had upon Roosevelt.

Time puts him on its cover.

The worldwide perception grows. Albert is responsible for the atomic bombs.

His own perceived involvement torments him. Newspapermen stop him in the street.

'Dr Einstein, Dr Einstein, d'you believe the atomic bomb will wipe out civilisation?'

'I do not believe that civilisation will be wiped out in a war fought with the atomic bomb.'

'How many people will be killed?'

'Perhaps two-thirds of the people of the Earth will be killed.'

'You must be so proud, Dr Einstein.'

'The unleashed power of the atom has changed everything save our modes of thinking and we thus drift toward unparalleled catastrophe.'

The Nobel Committee invites Albert to address the Fifth American Nobel Anniversary Dinner at the Hotel Astor in New York on 10 December 1945.

He takes the greatest care to compose a direct and simple speech that will not be misunderstood.

'Ladies and gentlemen, the Nobel Anniversary celebration takes on a special significance this year. Well, after our deadly struggle of many years, we are at peace again; or what we are supposed to consider as peace. And it bears a still more significant significance for the physicists who, in one way or another, were connected with the construction of the use of the atomic bomb.

'For these physicists find themselves in a position not unlike to that of Alfred Nobel himself.'

He explains that Nobel invented the most powerful explosive ever known, 'a means of destruction par excellence. In order to atone for this, in order to relieve his human conscience, he instituted his awards for the promotion of peace and for achievements of peace.'

He suggests that the physicists of today are harassed by an equal sense of guilt.

'We helped in creating this new weapon in order to prevent the enemies of mankind from achieving it ahead of us, which, given the mentality of the Nazis, would have meant inconceivable destruction and the enslavement of the rest of the world.

The physicists handed the weapon to the Americans and the British people as trustees of the whole [of] mankind, as fighters for peace and liberty. But so far, we fail to see any guarantee of peace. We do not see any guarantee of the freedoms that were promised to the nations in the Atlantic Charter. The war is won, but the peace is not . . .

The world was promised freedom from want, but large parts of the world are faced with starvation while others are living in abundance . . .

Allow me to be more specific about just one case, which is but a symptom of the general situation: the case of my own people, the Jewish people. As long as Nazi violence was unleashed only, or mainly, against the Jews, the rest of the world looked on passively; and even treaties and agreements were made with the patently criminal government of the Third Reich . . .

But after all that had happened, and was not prevented from happening – how is it today? . . .

. . . It is sheer irony when the British Foreign Minister tells the poor lot of European Jews they should remain in Europe because their genius is needed there, and, on the other hand, advises them not to try to get at the head of the queue lest they might incur new

191

hatred – hatred and persecution. Well, I am afraid they cannot help it; with their six million dead they have been pushed at the head of the queue, of the queue of Nazi victims, most against their will . . .

The situation calls for a courageous effort, for a radical change in our whole attitude in the entire political concept. May the spirit that prompted Alfred Nobel to create this great institution – the spirit of trust and confidence, of generosity and brotherhood among men – prevail in the minds of those upon whose decisions our destiny rests. Otherwise, human civilisation will be doomed.'

Albert mourns for the 140,000 dead at Hiroshima and 74,000 at Nagasaki. Atomic energy has been put to terrifying use.

The public believes uranium is a devastating explosive, that radiation and fallout are the same. History has shown Einstein that once an incorrect paradigm is created in the public mind, it can take over a hundred years for the incorrect paradigm to be dismissed and replaced by a more correct understanding.

He writes to *The New York Times*, quoting Roosevelt: 'We are faced with the pre-eminent fact that if civilisation is to survive we must cultivate the science of human relationship – the ability of peoples of all kinds to live together and work together in the same world, at peace. We have learned, and paid an awful price to learn, that living and working together can be done in one way only – under law. Unless it prevails, and unless by common struggle we are capable of new ways of thinking, mankind is doomed.'

Newsweek says:

Through the incomparable blast and flame that will follow, there will be dimly discernible to those who are interested in cause and effect in history, the features of a shy, almost saintly, childlike little man with the soft brown eyes, the drooping facial lines of a world-weary hound, and hair like an aurora borealis. Albert Einstein did not work directly on the atomic bomb. But Einstein was the father of the bomb in two important ways: 1) it was his initiative which started US bomb research; 2) it was his equation E = mc^2 which made the atomic bomb theoretically possible.

'Had I known that the Germans would not succeed in producing an atomic bomb, I would have never lifted a finger.'

Albert closes the door to the reporters.

Mileva, in Zürich, has weakened. Tete is still confined to a mental institution. The money Albert gave her from his Nobel Prize winnings has diminished. In May 1948, aged seventy-eight, she dies alone. Beneath her bed is a package containing 85,000 francs.

Albert complains of severe stomach pains. Doctors diagnose an aneurysm in his abdominal aorta. He goes with Helen Dukas to Sarasota, south of Tampa on Florida's Gulf Coast, to rest and regain strength.

Albert's sister, Maja, joins him in Princeton. She emigrated to the United States in 1939, although her husband's poor health prevented him from joining her. He remains with relatives in Geneva, where he dies in 1952. Maja lives with Albert at Mercer Street, but in 1946 suffers a stroke and arteriosclerosis and is bedridden.

Maja dies in 1951, aged seventy.

Albert continues to attend the Institute. His colleagues care for him and he's delighted when they give him a present, an AM-FM radio and record player.

His hair is now completely white and more untruly than ever. The lines in his face are deep. His eyes are watery. His fingers are so stiff he can no more play his violin.

He writes to Max Born: 'I am generally regarded as a sort of petrified object . . . I find this role not too distasteful, as it corresponds very well with my temperament . . . Giving is more enjoyable than receiving. It's best not to take myself nor the doings of the masses seriously, not to be ashamed of my weaknesses and vices, and naturally take things as they come with equanimity and humour.'

Embassy of Israel
Washington DC

November 17, 1952

Dear Professor Einstein,

The bearer of this letter is Dr David Goitein of Jerusalem who is now serving as Minister of our Embassy in Washington. He is bringing you the question which Prime Minister Ben Gurion asked me to convey to you, namely, whether you would accept the Presidency of Israel if it were offered to you by a vote of the Knesset. Acceptance would entail moving to Israel and taking its citizenship. The Prime Minister assures me that in such circumstances complete facility and freedom to pursue your great scientific work would be afforded by a government and people who are fully conscious of the supreme significance of your labors.

Mr Goitein will be able to give you any information that you may desire on the implications of the Prime Minister's question.

Whatever your inclination or decision may be, I should be deeply grateful for an opportunity to speak with you again within the next day or two at any place convenient for you. I understand the anxieties and doubts which you expressed to me this evening. On the other hand, whatever your answer, I am anxious for you to feel that the Prime Minister's question embodies the deepest respect which the Jewish people can repose in any of its sons. To this element of personal regard, we add the sentiment that Israel is a small State in its physical dimensions, but can rise to the level of greatness in the measure that it exemplifies the most elevated spiritual and intellectual traditions which the Jewish people has established through its best minds and hearts both in antiquity and in modern times. Our first President, as you know, taught us to see our destiny in these great perspectives, as you yourself have often exhorted us to do.

Therefore, whatever your response to this question, I hope that you will think generously of those who have asked it, and will commend the high purposes and motives which prompted them to think of you at this solemn hour in our people's history.

With cordial wishes,

Abba Eban

To which Albert replies:

I am deeply moved by the offer from our State of Israel, and at once saddened and ashamed that I cannot accept it. All my life I have dealt with objective matters, hence I lack both the natural aptitude and the experience to deal properly with people and to exercise official functions. For these reasons alone I should be unsuited to fulfill the duties of that high office, even if advancing age was not making increasing inroads on my strength. I am the more distressed over these circumstances because my relationship to the Jewish people has become my strongest human bond, ever since I became fully aware of our precarious situation among the nations of the world.

GANDHI

Twenty years have passed since the Nazi gangs lit bonfires of books in front of the Berlin Opera House. Among others the books of Mann, Zweig, Remarque, Gide, Hemingway, Heine, Freud, Marx, Wedekind, Nabokov, Tolstoy. Einstein.

The Un-American Activities Committee doesn't summon Albert. But Albert is keen to pick a fight with the inquisitors.

He gets his chance when he receives a letter from a Brooklyn English teacher, William Frauenglass. The Senate Internal Security Subcommittee has subpoenaed Frauenglass because six years ago he gave a lecture entitled 'Techniques of Intercultural Teaching in the Field of English as a Means of Overcoming Prejudice Among School Children'. Frauenglass has refused to testify, which means that the New York City School Board will sack him. He writes to Albert for assistance, which will be 'most helpful in rallying educators and the public to resist this new obscurantist attack'.

Albert's reply is published in *The New York Times*:

The problem with which the intellectuals of this country are confronted is very serious. The reactionary politicians have managed to instil suspicion of all intellectual efforts into the public by dangling before their eyes a danger from without. Having succeeded so far, they are now proceeding to suppress the freedom of teaching and to deprive of their positions all those who do not prove submissive, i.e., to starve them. What ought the minority of intellectuals to do against this evil? Frankly, I can see only the revolutionary way of non-cooperation in the sense of Gandhi's. Every intellectual who is called before one of the committees ought to refuse to testify, i.e., he must be prepared for jail and economic ruin, in short, for the sacrifice of his personal welfare in the interest of the cultural welfare of this country. This refusal to testify must be based on the assertion that it is shameful for a blameless citizen to submit to such an inquisition and that this kind of inquisition violates the spirit of the Constitution. If enough people are ready to take this grave step they will be successful. If not, then the intellectuals of this country deserve nothing better than the slavery which is intended for them.

Senator McCarthy calls Albert 'an enemy of the American people'. The *Washington Post* warns that if 'citizens generally followed Dr Einstein's advice and went to jail in preference to testifying, our representative system would be paralysed. If we are going to have orderly government, each summoned witness must be required to speak.'

Albert by now is too weary and frail to be called. He sits in his study packing tobacco into his pipe, lighting it, relighting it. The cloud of smoke rises above his head.

FIVE

KURT GÖDEL

Outside 112 Mercer Street, a sinister, gaunt, buttoned-up man stands staring at the closed shutters.

The man is five feet six inches tall and wears a white linen suit and matching fedora. His face is owlish. Heavy pebble glasses magnify his piercing blue eyes.

He dithers about on the lawn in front of the house, counting and recounting out loud the steps to the veranda. Then the dozen red roses he's carrying with a card attached: 'To my dearest friend, A.E. Happy Birthday. Kurt Gödel.'

A uniformed chauffeur drives Mimi and Isabella Beaufort to St David's High School in a Chrysler Crown Imperial Limousine.

The sisters are tall and slim. Both have full heads of fair hair in a high ponytail tied with a silk scarf. They wear shirtwaist polka-dot dresses, white ankle socks and sandals.

They settle back in the plush upholstered seats and catch up with the latest correspondence from their widowed father, Whitney Beaufort, who rambles on as usual about Beaufort Park in Greenwich, Connecticut, where a succession of nannies raised Mimi and Isabella in the mansion known as the Fort.

The reclusive Whitney Beaufort is now a frail figure, wheelchair-bound with rheumatoid arthritis and the premature onset of dementia. A butler and nurses attend to his every need. He only appears at dinnertime, when he eats in silence. The staff includes an elderly chauffeur along with gardeners, cooks and kitchen maids. Other than to bathe, dress and be lifted into his wheelchair to appear for the silent dinners, Whitney Beaufort stays in bed.

Before the second war a procession of notables stayed at the Fort with the Beauforts, including Franklin Roosevelt when he was governor of New York.

Another regular guest was the founder of Mimi and Isabella's school, the eccentric Harvard scholar Avery Whittingale III. To FDR's pleasure, Whittingale declaimed the comic verse of Edmund Clerihew Bentley, particularly Beaufort's favourite: 'Geoffrey Chaucer / Could hardly have been coarser, / But this never harmed the sales / Of his Canterbury Tales.'

International scholars of medieval literature visit the Beaufort Library to peer at the early fifteenth-century illuminated manuscript of *The Canterbury Tales*. Art historians come to the mansion to inspect the Beaufort *Venus of Urbino*, the painting of a woman who bears a striking resemblance to the model Titian employed for *La Bella* in the Pitti Palace in Florence, the *Girl in a Fur* in Vienna and the *Woman with a Plumed Hat* in St Petersburg.

Alas, the Chaucer manuscript and Titian were sold in 1939. The paintings remaining on the walls of the Fort are doubtful examples of 1920s American regionalism: minor paintings by Grant Wood, John Steuart Curry, Thomas Hart Benton and an early Andrew Wyeth.

Most of the books and prints in the library have suffered from damp. The library catalogue was loaned to an auction house in New York City and has subsequently vanished. By the late 1940s Beaufort Park, like the school Mimi and Isabella attend, has fallen into a state of decrepitude.

The Beaufort family is snobbish. If grand-sounding names are raised in family conversation someone asks: 'Who are *they* . . . ? Did *they* go to St David's or Harvard or Yale?' Family blood, ties, names, grand houses and estates, the recognition of Society, unspoken fortunes and ancestry is what matters.

The girls' father had always intended they should attend St David's in Princeton. What Whitney Beaufort's lawyers keep secret is the parlous state of the family's finances. In short, money is fast running out.

Mimi and Isabella might dream of studying at the Royal Academy of Music in London. Unfortunately there are insufficient funds to enable them to do so. Meanwhile, the family lawyers have made some sort of provision with the bank to meet the fees at St David's.

During term-time the sisters – Mimi seventeen years old and Isabella a year younger – lodge outside Princeton at their Uncle Bradley's house, where his housekeeper and servants care for them. It is from there that Mimi made the morning call to Einstein by mistake.

Uncle Bradley Beaufort is rarely there. He enjoys a close personal friendship with the Eisenhowers and has some hush-hush executive position in Washington with the CIA, liaising with the White House.

En route to St David's, Mimi lowers her voice. 'Isabella – can you keep a secret? This is the truth. I just spoke with Albert Einstein.'

'You what?'

'I just spoke with Albert Einstein.'

'Are you crazy?'

'I did. It's true.'

'Einstein – c'mon – Einstein? *The* Einstein?'

'I promise. I was dialling the pharmacy. I got the wrong number. And this voice says, "Albert Einstein speaking." His number is 341 2400. The pharmacy's is 341 2499.'

Isabella is wide-eyed. 'You spoke to Albert Einstein?'

'Sure – I spoke to Einstein,' Mimi says.

'What's he like?'

'Real friendly. German accent. With a voice that's kind of about to laugh. Today's his birthday. He's seventy-five.'

'That's a wonderful thing,' says Isabella, who relishes the fact that 'wonderful things' are always happening around Mimi.

In one of the high-ceilinged, damp music rooms, Mimi and Isabella practise the second movement of Mozart's Sonata for Piano and Violin in E minor, K.304.

At its end, Isabella says, 'That's good – one more time?'

'We have to go,' says Mimi. 'Physics. You forgotten? $E = mc^2$.'

'Haven't I told you a hundred times – I still don't get it,' Isabella says. 'Sorry. I just don't.'

'What's wrong with you, Isabella?'

'It's tough to understand. Let's stick to music.'

The same morning, a few minutes after ten o'clock, Albert and his devoted companion Kurt Gödel, the strange, gaunt figure who's been waiting outside the house on Mercer Street with the bouquet of roses, stroll through the streets in animated conversation.

As usual, the walk to the Princeton Institute for Advanced Study takes them half an hour. They reel off the names of the flowers they see.

'Forsythia, star magnolias, espaliered saucer magnolia. Pink, purple, white flowers,' says Einstein.

'Cherry blossom, tulips soon, daffodils, witch hazel, flowering dogwood,' says Gödel.

'God's work,' Albert says. 'God's work.'

'God's work,' says Gödel.

Their colleagues at the Institute recognise that the strange-looking friends walk and talk on equal terms. There's wildness and other worldliness about Gödel's genius that fascinates Albert. Gödel can manipulate the most arcane philosophical and mathematical concepts. For his part, Albert – Jew, pacifist, socialist, scientist-philosopher – is the one man Gödel looks up to.

Only when it comes to artistic tastes is there a certain parting of the ways. Albert of course adores Mozart and Bach. Gödel, the work of Walt Disney.

Yet they share their thinking about the universe of space-time, the fourth dimension. And Gödel also believes that the distribution of matter is such that the structure of space-time is curved and warped.

Thus, a spacecraft travelling fast enough can reach any region of the past, present or future.

Born in Brünn in Austria-Hungary, Gödel studied in Vienna and was appointed *Privatdozent* by the university. In the 1930s, the Nazis terminated Gödel's post, believing his politics to be 'doubtful'. A new position would be awarded if Gödel passed 'a political test'.

The Nazis were also suspicious of the three visits Gödel had paid to the United States.

In 1936, a fanatical Nazi student assassinates his mentor, Moritz Schlick, on the steps of Vienna University, which leads Gödel to develop a paranoid fear of assassination.

Three years later, the Nazis declare Gödel fit for military service, prompting Gödel and his wife, Adele, to flee.

They travel on the Trans-Siberian Railway to Japan, then by ship to San Francisco, where they arrive in March 1940.

They finally settle in Princeton, where Gödel's position at the Institute for Advanced Study is annually renewed until 1946, when he becomes a permanent member and is subsequently appointed to the faculty.

He becomes an American citizen in 1948, declaring to those officiating at the ceremony that he finds logical inconsistencies in the US Constitution. Albert, a witness, has to tell him to shut up, and finally diverts him by telling worn-out jokes.

Once in Princeton, Gödel's acute hypochondria plagues him: fears which originate from his childhood attacks of rheumatic fever, and that bring on two nervous breakdowns and increasing isolation.

Adele is his helpmate. Gödel met her aged twenty-one in Vienna, when she was a twenty-seven-year-old dancer in the nightclub *Der Nachtfalter* (The Moth), on Petersplatz. Adele was a Catholic divorcée.

A birthmark disfigured her face. Gödel's parents viewed the love-match with alarm and despair.

Gödel, obsessed with the idea that the gasses from the refrigerator and central-heating system are poisoning his food, seems to retreat from life. He watches Walt Disney's *Snow White* on his Kodak Kodascope 16mm Pageant Sound Projector over and over again, avoids social contact, and engages in long nocturnal telephone conversations with anyone who'll listen.

He insists that Adele feed him butter, baby food and Fletcher's Castoria laxative. She tries to divert his gloom by arranging to house a pink flamingo in their front yard on Linden Lane. Gödel mutters that the creature is awfully charming.

Adele is more than content that her husband has a place at the Institute that she dubs the old pensioners' home.

Only with Albert does Gödel seem to regain a sort of equilibrium. Albert is the world's most famous scientist. Gödel is the greatest logician of his generation, though his name means nothing to the world at large.

Their route this morning in the beautiful spring of 1954 takes them through the neighbourhood that only infrequently sees whites. The black locals recognise Albert and smile at him with affection and he returns their smiles. Residents pause to watch him buy an ice cream on Nassau Street.

A small black boy runs up to Albert brandishing an album. 'Can I have your autograph, please?'

'Do you know who I am?' Albert asks.

'You look like Dr Einstein.'

Albert relights his pipe. 'That is correct. Let me see whose autographs you have.' He opens the autograph album. 'Ah, yes. Look, Gödel.'

Gödel looks at the signature: *Tony Galento.*

'The heavyweight prizefighter,' Albert announces. 'Two Ton Tony Galento. He lives in Orange, New Jersey. Five feet eight inches tall. Two hundred and forty pounds in weight. Two Ton Tony.'

'It is incorrect to say he weighs two tons,' Gödel observes.

'The Noble Art is one of exaggeration,' Albert says. 'Galento won a ten-dollar wager by eating fifty-two hot dogs before fighting Arthur DeKuh in '32. They had to slit Galento's boxing shorts to make them fit. Then he knocked out DeKuh in four rounds.'

Albert and the boy laugh uproariously.

'Look, Gödel – the autograph of Jerry Lewis. Do you know who he is?'

'No.'

'And Frank Sinatra. You know of Sinatra?'

'He won the Academy Award for Best Supporting Actor for playing Private Angelo Maggio in *From Here to Eternity.*'

Gödel imitates Sinatra's Private Angelo: '"Let's go to a phone booth or something, huh? Where I will unveil a fifth of whiskey I have hidden here under my loose, flowing sports shirt."'

'Like, crazy,' the boy says. 'Like, wow!'

Gödel begins to sing 'There's No Business Like Show Business' in his heavy German accent.

Albert joins in and they dance and sing together.

'Extraordinary,' Albert says. 'Where did you learn that?'

'With Adele. At Der Nachtfalter. My grandfather Joseph was a singer, a member of the Brünner Männergesangverein.'

'Glee club?' says Albert. 'Bravo. A glee club, full of glee.'

Gödel's face darkens. 'There are other worlds and rational beings of a different and higher kind. The world in which we live is not the only one in which we shall live or have lived.'

'D'you guys have a pen?' the boy says.

'I do,' says Albert. 'But if you're going to be a serious autograph collector you must always carry a pen.'

Albert produces his black Waterman 22 Taper fountain pen. 'Here. This is my laboratory.'

'I thought you'd given it to Paul Ehrenfest in Leiden?' Gödel says.

'That was the Waterman I first wrote $E = mc^2$ with.'

Albert happily signs his autograph and, stooping down, fishes out a nickel from his pocket and gives it to the boy.

The laughing boy ruffles Albert's mop of hair.

'You should ask my friend Professor Gödel here for his autograph,' Albert says.

'Why?'

'Because Kurt Gödel's work on the foundation of mathematics has changed the world we live in.'

'Did he make a bomb?'

'No, he did not.'

'Is he a genius like you?'

'He is a genius. Yes. Whether, like me, he understands the entire universe, from the greatest galaxy to the tiniest elementary particle, I do not know. Whether, like me, he will find the principles that cover everything in a unified field theory, we shall see . . .'

'OK,' the boy says. 'Sign here, Kurt.'

Gödel signs his name, adding: '$2 + 2 = 4$'.

'I know that,' the boy says.

'That makes you a mathematical genius too then,' Gödel pronounces.

'Crazy,' the boy says. 'You guys are a big tickle.'

As the boy hands back the fountain pen he triggers the ink release and black ink squirts across Albert's hands.

'You can keep it,' Albert says, laughing and wiping his hands on his handkerchief.

The boy runs off waving the autograph album and the fountain pen in the air in triumph.

Albert and Gödel walk on.

'I feel a kinship with the oppressed,' Albert says. 'Perhaps they will inherit the Earth and join us in the hereafter. Tell me, Kurt. Do you believe in the hereafter?'

'I do. Yes. There's got to be another world beyond the present.'

'Why?'

'Why not?' asks Gödel. 'What would be the reason for creating man if he were allowed to achieve one in the thousands of things that he's capable of achieving? Look, you and I arrived on Earth clueless about why we'd arrived or where we'd come from. Who dares say we'll depart in any equally clueless way? In all probability the Earth will end anyway.'

'A knowledge of the existence of something we cannot penetrate,' says Albert, 'of the manifestations of the profoundest reason and the most radiant beauty – it is this knowledge and this emotion that constitute the truly religious attitude; in this sense, and in this alone, I am a deeply religious man.'

'Like I say, the world will end anyway.'

'Of course,' says Albert, taken aback by the intensity of Gödel's view of the probability of the end of the Earth.

'I believe we'll enter the next world with memories of this world and basic matters will be preserved with certainty. Do you know the most widely known equation?'

'$E = mc^2$?'

'No,' says Gödel. 'It's $2 + 2 = 4$.'

'Ha ha,' says Albert. '"For Thine is . . ."'

'"Life is . . ."' Gödel says.

'"For Thine is the . . ."' says Albert.

Together, dancing up and down, they chant: '"This is the way the world ends. This is the way the world ends. This is the way the world ends. Not with a bang but a whimper."'

Breathless, Albert says: 'Be honest with me, Kurt Gödel, are you eating?'

Gödel gives a high-pitched chuckle.

'It's not funny, Doktor Gödel.'

'You eat for comfort,' Gödel says, 'because you have failed to find a unified field theory to bring together quantum mechanics with general relativity.'

'You don't believe in it?' Albert says.

'No.'

'Why not?'

'Because I don't believe in natural science,' Gödel says. 'All it's achieved is TV and bombs. You don't believe in mathematics?'

Albert hoiks up the suspenders of his baggy pants. 'I believe in intuition.'

'God?' Gödel says.

'God doesn't consult with me,' Albert says. 'Unfortunately. Why is the universe expanding over time, huh? It really is expanding. There exists a new space-time.'

Gödel stares at the sky. 'We live in a world in which ninety-nine per cent of all beautiful things are destroyed. The world doesn't understand. The world doesn't understand a word we say.'

'Is that why you aren't eating, Kurt?'

'I'm not eating because my medications are incorrect. Because my doctors can't write. They'll commit me to a psychiatric hospital. My grave will be housed in a lunatic asylum. And yours?'

'My grave,' Albert says, 'will be a place of pilgrimage.'

Gödel laughs. 'Where pilgrims will come to view the bones of a saint?'

'Yes,' says Albert. 'What will become of your bodily remains, Kurt?'

Gödel chuckles. 'I am going to be cremated for 90 minutes at a temperature of 760 to 1,150 degrees Celsius. There'll be no headstone. No "Rest in Peace". *Requiescat in pace.* How do we know we'll rest in peace? I trust mathematics. I mistrust language.'

'And no one trusts either of us,' Albert says. 'Here in Princeton I'm known as the village idiot. What is it you really want, Kurt?'

'To be remembered as the man who discovered you can't trust language. And you?'

'Not to be remembered as the man who invented the atomic bomb. You know the greatest mistake I ever made?'

'Tell me,' says Gödel.

'Signing that letter to President Roosevelt advocating that the bomb be built.'

'You can be forgiven. There was the high probability the Germans were working on the problem and they might succeed and use the hideous weapon to become the master race. So what'll you do now?'

'Send a note to Bertrand Russell in England. Russell can publish what we think needs to be done. '"Shall we put an end to the human race; or shall mankind renounce war? People will not face this alternative because it is so difficult to abolish war." Is it ignoble to try and prevent the destruction of life on Earth?'

Outside the Institute, Gödel is suddenly distracted by the tall, very thin, frowning figure of a man.

'My, oh my,' Gödel whispers. 'I spy with my little eye. Someone beginning with O.'

'I thought he was on St John in the Virgin Islands,' Albert says.

211

'May I wish you a happy birthday?' Oppenheimer says.

'Thank you, my dear director.'

The tall and patrician Oppenheimer, born the year before Albert produced $E = mc^2$, hands Albert a package. 'Come to my office at lunchtime for a celebratory drink. You too, Kurt.'

'May we expect one of your world-famous martinis?' Gödel asks.

'You may indeed,' says Oppenheimer, going about his business.

Several students pause outside the Institute's entrance to watch the encounter.

Albert opens the birthday package Oppenheimer's given him. It contains a copy of the *Bhagavad Gita*.

Oppenheimer has inserted a book mark inscribed: 'The <u>battle lines</u> apply to us. Happy Birthday to the greatest of scientists. J.R.O.'

Albert reads: 'In battle, in the forest, at the precipice in the mountains, / On the dark great sea, in the midst of javelins and arrows, / In sleep, in confusion, in the depths of shame, / The good deeds a man has done before defend him.'

When Albert and Gödel enter the Institute a crowd of students and faculty members break into spontaneous applause. Many have cameras and photograph Albert.

Retaining both his composure and humour, Albert does what the student photographers hope, just what he did on his seventy-second birthday when the United Press International photographer Arthur Sasse struggled to persuade Albert to allow yet one more birthday photo at the Princeton Club: he sticks out his tongue.

The students and faculty members cheer and break into a deafening rendering of 'Happy Birthday To You'.

JOHANNA

In the afternoon, Johanna Fantova calls at Mercer Street to trim Albert's hair.

The pair have been friends since the 1920s. Johanna, born in Czechoslovakia, twenty years younger than Einstein, has been map curator in the Princeton Library since the early 1950s and, in addition to Frau Dukas, acts part-time as Albert's private assistant and secretary.

Albert relishes the care with which Johanna combs and cuts the mass of his white unruly hair and trims his moustache. Tufts of it collect on the sheet she's draped across his shoulders. Her attentions seem to increase his loquacity.

'I attract every lunatic on Earth. I feel sorry for these people. There's a woman requesting half a dozen autographs to leave to her children because she has nothing else to leave them.'

'Do you believe her?'

'No. But let's send them anyway. And there's a physicist saying I'm a mathematician and a mathematician saying I'm a physicist. Maybe Joseph McCarthy and his Committee will let me know what I am. I'm sick of their persecution of Oppenheimer. Why not look at what Heisenberg did for Hitler?'

'Heisenberg's a good pianist.'

'About as good a pianist as Hitler was a painter.'

'Heisenberg wants to visit you.'

'Ha ha. I will be out.'

'So does Niels Bohr's son.'

'Aage Bohr is nicer than Heisenberg but talks too much.'

Ignoring Johanna's hair cutting, Albert swivels round to the piano.

'I live my daydreams in music. I see my life in terms of music.'

'I know.'

'Do you? Listen—'

He starts playing Mozart's Piano Sonata No. 16 in C major, K.545. 'I get most joy in life out of music.'

Johanna listens, her head swaying to the music, like Albert in rapture.

Frau Dukas has her hands full at Mercer Street.

She fusses over the arrangements for the evening concert, just like the one in 1952, when the Juilliard Quartet played Bartok, Beethoven and Mozart. Albert had been invited to join in.

For this evening's concert, he has another idea up his sleeve. With Frau Dukas out of earshot he lifts the telephone and dials the number on Born's letter.

Mimi Beaufort answers.

'Mimi?'

'Yes.'

'Albert Einstein speaking.'

'I hoped it might be. I want to wish you happy birthday.'

'Why, thank you. Thank you, Mimi.'

'How are you doing, Dr Einstein?'

'Considering that I've triumphantly survived Nazism and two wives, I'm doing just fine. What've you been doing?'

'Playing music.'

'What music?'

'The second movement of Mozart's Sonata for Piano and Violin in E minor, K.304.

'Do you have your violin close by?'

'Sure,' says Mimi.

'Can you play it for me?'

'Sure I can.'

Albert listens in ecstasy. 'Bravo,' he cries. 'Bravo.' In high excitement he gabbles on. 'You must come and see me ten days from now. Some fine musicians are coming to give a little birthday concert for me. I want you to be here. Will you come and play for me?'

'Sure. What time?'

'Seven-thirty – you know my address?'

'Sure – I looked it up in the directory.'

'Do you like ice cream?'

'Sure I do.'

'Me too. We'll play Mozart and have ice cream.'

'Can I bring my sister, Isabella? Can we play that Mozart sonata?'

Albert leaves his study and goes in search of Frau Dukas. He finds her in the kitchen. 'I'll be out for a couple of hours,' he tells her.

'Where?'

'At the Institute with Gödel,' Albert says. 'You must prepare for the party. I mustn't get in your way. Oh, and yes, Helen – I'll be seeing

215

your fellow executor of my will, Otto Nathan. Please be sure to see we have a plentiful supply of ice cream for tonight's guests.'

Einstein leaves the house and walks along Mercer Street conducting his singing of Mozart's 'Eine kleine Nachtmusik': '*Da*-da-*da* da-*da*-da-*da*-da-*da*! *Da*-da-*da* da-*da*-da-*da*-da-*da*!'

He pays no attention to the black Ford Tudor Sedan, whose driver and passenger give him cursory glances.

The two men wait for him to disappear from sight before making their way to the front door of Albert's house.

Frau Dukas answers the door to the callers.

She thinks maybe they're Christian Scientists or Jehovah's Witnesses, or from the Church of Scientology.

One of them, bull-necked, grins, showing yellow teeth. 'May we take up a few moments of your time?'

'I'm afraid I have my hands full,' Frau Dukas says.

'You're Helen Dukas?' the second man says.

'I am, yes. How can I be of help?'

'You're Dr Einstein's secretary and housekeeper?'

'Yes, I am. Dr Einstein isn't here at the moment. Would you like to make an appointment to see him?'

'Matter of fact,' the first man says, 'it's you we'd like to talk to.'

'Me . . . ? What do you want to talk to me about? Who are you?'

Both men produce black wallets containing their identification as Federal Bureau of Investigation special agents from the FBI office in Newark, New Jersey. Special Agent John Ruggiero and Special Agent Jan Grzeskiewicz.

'FBI?' says Frau Dukas. 'Is something wrong?'

'Nothing's wrong, Frau Dukas,' says the yellow-toothed Ruggiero. 'We'd just like a moment's help clarifying a few facts.'

'Very well. If it won't take long. You'd better come inside.'

'If we can talk in private?' says Grzeskiewicz.

She leads the two men into Albert's study.

Grzeskiewicz turns his back to Frau Dukas and his companion. Reaching inside his jacket he activates a small recording device. A Protona Minifon. His watch has a microphone built into it. Ruggiero produces a notebook and ballpoint pen. He asks the questions:

'You've been in Dr Einstein's employ since 1928?'

'Yes, I have.'

'As secretary and housekeeper?'

'Yes. Before that Dr Einstein's wife acted in those capacities, as well as cook.'

'Elsa. In Berlin?'

'Elsa, yes,' says Frau Dukas. 'Some twenty-five years ago. In Berlin. And now Dr Einstein is seventy-five. He is frail. He has a bad heart. Meanwhile I have a job to do, gentlemen.'

'So do we, ma'am,' says Ruggiero with a laugh. He produces a pack of Camels.

'You want a cigarette?'

'No,' says Frau Dukas.

Ruggiero lights up a cigarette. 'We have orders to ask you if you are acquainted with or have ever heard of Georgi Mikhailovich Dimitrov. What d'you know of him?'

'Dimitrov? That he was accused along with other Communists of plotting the Reichstag fire. He was acquitted.'

Ruggiero reads from his notebook. 'Dimitrov settled in Moscow and, as secretary-general of the Comintern's executive committee, encouraged the formation of popular-front movements against the Nazis except when Stalin was co-operating with Adolf Hitler. During 1944 he directed the resistance to Bulgaria's Axis satellite government, and in 1945 he returned to Bulgaria, where he was immediately appointed prime minister of a Communist-dominated Fatherland Front government. Assuming dictatorial control of political affairs, he effected the Communist consolidation of power that culminated in the formation of the People's Republic of Bulgaria in 1946. He called upon Dr Einstein in Berlin.'

'I have no recollection of that. Anyhow Dr Einstein had few callers and handled his affairs by mail.'

'You have copies of Dr Einstein's correspondence?'

'None that's available.'

'You're interested in politics, Frau Dukas?'

'Only that I was against the rise of Hitler in Germany. My circle of friends was Jewish. I was interested first and foremost in Jewish affairs. My interests in life are Jewish affairs and Dr Einstein. Are you suggesting that Dr Einstein has Communist sympathies?'

'Do you think that's a fair assumption?' Ruggiero asks with a tone of apology.

'No, I don't.'

'D'you agree, Frau Dukas, that with the passage of time, your mind isn't too clear?'

'About what?'

'Names, dates, places,' says Ruggiero. 'To do with Dr Einstein's life in Berlin from 1928 to 1933. We've evidence that Dr Einstein's senior secretary, Elsa Einstein, or his elder stepdaughter had contacts with Soviet couriers.'

'His stepdaughter served as his secretary until 1926 when she married. She's dead. So is Elsa.'

'You recall Dr Einstein's apartment?'

'Naturally.'

'With a pair of entrances and exits. The main staircase led out on to Haberlandstrasse. And the other staircase?'

'The servants' staircase led on to Aschaffenburger Strasse.'

'Perfect for couriers to come and go without bring observed?'

'If you say so. It never crossed my mind.'

'It's crossed mine,' says Ruggiero. 'It was because of Dr Einstein's failing health in March 1928 he had to employ a new secretary. Elsa Einstein talked to your sister, Rosa, of the Jewish Orphan Organisation. Rosa recommended you. And you went to 5 Haberlandstrasse on Friday 13 April 1928 to be interviewed.'

'Yes. And I planned to refuse the appointment.'

'Why?'

'Because I knew nothing of physics.'

'But you had contact with Communists?'

'I certainly did not.'

'But your brother-in-law Sigmund Wollenberger was a Communist – likewise his nephew, Albert Wollenberger. When Dr Einstein came to the United States Wollenberger's aunt acted as sponsor. And Dr Einstein's involvement in numerous Communist organisations was known inside Germany and beyond. He was a trustee of the Red Aid children's homes, the Society of Friends of the New Russia, the International Workers Relief, and the World Committee against Imperialistic War.'

'Maybe. I don't recall.'

'You say Dr Einstein has never been a Communist?'

'He definitely has not.'

'Or an anti-Communist?'

'Maybe not.'

'And you?'

'The same.'

'You're not anti-Communist?'

Frau Dukas stays silent.

Ruggiero turns to the soundman, Grzeskiewicz. 'D'you have any questions?'

'Nope,' says Grzeskiewicz.

'OK, Frau Dukas,' says Ruggiero. 'Thank you for your co-operation. You've been most kind.'

'You're welcome.'

'May I have your solemn word that this meeting will remain confidential?'

'If it doesn't?'

'You will be arrested under the provision of the Espionage Act. The reputation of Dr Einstein will be destroyed. You wouldn't want to go the way of the Rosenbergs, would you?'

Frau Dukas fights to control her rage. '*Have you forgotten?* Have you forgotten that Sartre called the trial a legal lynching which smeared a whole nation with blood?'

'Dr Einstein protested too, didn't he, Frau Dukas? So did Bertolt Brecht, Dashiell Hammett, Frida Kahlo.'

'*I think you'd better leave,*' Frau Dukas says.

'Then, Frau Dukas, don't you mention this visit, see?' says Ruggiero. 'It didn't happen, OK?'

Frau Dukas shows them to the door in silence.

'Good day, Frau Dukas,' Ruggiero says.

She is fearful and makes no reply. For a while she stands watching them ambling to their Ford looking very pleased with themselves.

The FBI agents don't leave Mercer Street straight away.

Ruggiero turns to Grzeskiewicz. 'You thinking what I'm thinking?'

'That she told us a whole heap of shit?'

'Yes.'

'That's what I'm thinking, buddy.'

Grzeskiewicz removes the recording device, rewinds the tape and makes a random selection to check the device has worked.

'*My interests in life are Jewish affairs and Dr Einstein. Are you suggesting that Dr Einstein has Communist sympathies?*'

'Yes, he does,' says Ruggiero as he starts the car and drives away. 'We got him – they can prepare the cell.'

'Old Sparky?' Grzeskiewicz chuckles.

'I guess so.'

'You ever see Old Sparky in action?'

'Sure,' says Ruggiero. 'Man strapped in. Gets to say his last words. Whir of exhaust fan in the execution chamber. Big, big bang and the guy convulses for around fifteen seconds. They send another wave through him. It's done to condemn outrageous offences against humanity. People need to know history.'

'What were the guy's last words?'

'I forget.'

'What d'you reckon Einstein's will be?'

'Dunno,' says Grzeskiewicz.

'Maybe $E = mc^2$?'

'That's a gas. You could be right.'

'Do you know what that means?'

'$E = mc^2$?'

'What's it mean?'

'How the hell would I know?'

'Some kind of Jewish shit?'

'Jewish or Commie.'

'Same thing.'

'We nailed him.'

'He's nailed himself.'

'Like Christ.'

'Don't take it that far, buddy. This is the United States of America.'

*

221

On Wednesday morning, 24 March 1954, at the newly opened Ann Taylor's store on Palmer Square West, Mimi and Isabella choose their party dresses with care.

Mimi selects a black silk cocktail dress made of shantung satin. The skirt has crinoline sewn in behind the lining for fullness. There's a trim of ribbon along the bottom edge of the petticoat. She buys a pair of kitten heel, dark silver shoes.

'Grace Kelly?' says Mimi.

'Eva Marie Saint,' Isabella says. '*On the Waterfront*. Edie Doyle.'

Mimi helps Isabella select a floral dress.

'Who am I?' Isabella asks.

'Doris Day.'

'They are all so old,' Isabella says. 'We're more Audrey Hepburn.'

'"I might as well be reaching for the moon."'

'*Sabrina?*'

'*Sabrina.*'

MARIAN ANDERSON

Albert is in his element among his friends at the gathering in the music room on the ground floor at 112 Mercer Street.

On the Bechstein upright he accompanies the celebrated contralto Marian Anderson.

Two decades before, Anderson gave regular recitals across the nation. Encountering racial prejudice everywhere, she was forbidden from staying in hotel rooms and dining in restaurants. Albert loathed the discrimination against her. In 1937 she was denied a hotel room before performing at Princeton University, so Albert hosted her. There is now a rumour that she might receive an invitation to be the first African American to perform at the Metropolitan Opera House.

That evening for Albert she sings Schubert's 'Ave Maria'.

The audience applaud loudly.

No matter that most of them know who everyone is, Albert introduces his guests in turn:

'My stepdaughter, Margot. J. Robert Oppenheimer and his wife and children: Oppie and Kitty, Toni and Peter. Kurt and Adele Gödel. János Plesch, my doctor, his wife Melanie, and their children Andreas Odilo, Dagmar Honoria and Peter Hariolf. Dr Otto Nathan, co-executor of my will. Princeton's first African-American professor, Charles T. Davis, literary scholar and critic, and Jeanne and Anthony and Charles.

From Japan, Toichiro Kinoshita, theoretical physicist.

From Sweden, the mathematician Arne Carl-August Beurling, and Karin.

The art historian Erwin "Pan" Panofsky, and Dora and Wolfgang and Hans.

From China, the physicist Chen-Ning Franklin Yang and Chih-li Tu.

Johanna Fantova.

223

Mimi and Isabella Beaufort.'

Everyone applauds.

'My physician has instructed me not to play my violin tonight,' Albert chuckles. 'So Miss Mimi and Miss Isabella Beaufort will perform the second movement of Mozart's Sonata for Piano and Violin in E minor, K.304.'

Mimi and Isabella play the Mozart note perfect.

At the end the audience stand and applaud wildly.

Frau Dukas approaches Mimi and Isabella and hands them enormous bouquets of red roses.

Albert raises his arms asking for silence.

'I now invite the Beaufort sisters to play, unusually in partnership, the Andante from Mozart's Piano Concerto No. 21 in C major, K.467. The flute, two oboes, two bassoons, two horns, two trumpets, timpani and strings will accompany them.'

The orchestra take their rather cramped seats to more applause.

Albert assumes the role of conductor.

The music drifts across Mercer Street.

Seated listening on the sidewalk is the solitary figure of the small black boy clutching his autograph book and Albert's black Waterman 22 Taper fountain pen.

Again rapturous applause follows the performance.

Everyone takes their bows. Albert, Mimi and Isabella hold hands.

Once the applause subsides, Albert says quietly, 'Will you two visit me tomorrow?'

'Of course we will,' says Mimi. 'Can we by any chance go sailing with you one day?'

'I will have a little think,' says Albert. 'Can you two swim?'

'Sure,' says Mimi. 'Can you?'

'No,' says Albert. 'I never learned.'

Across the room Frau Dukas supervises the maids serving food from the buffet. Albert's favourite egg-drop soup. Asparagus. Filet de porc with sweet chestnuts. Salmon and mayonnaise. One whole table is set aside for strawberries, ice cream and meringues.

'We haven't been formally introduced,' Frau Dukas says to Isabella. 'I'm Helen Dukas, Dr Einstein's secretary. Your playing was beautiful.'

'Thank you.'

'Do you come from a musical family?'

'No,' says Isabella. 'If anything, we're military. My uncle, Bradley Beaufort, has some sort of secret job at Langley, Virginia, liaising with the White House. He's a pal of President Eisenhower's and the First Lady.'

'Ah,' a voice says. 'I'm Otto Nathan. I'm glad you two are getting to know Frau Dukas. She's my excellent co-trustee of Dr Einstein's will.'

'That's quite a responsibility,' says Mimi.

'Yes,' said Nathan. 'It is an honour.'

Mimi can't fathom why the heavily suited Nathan mentions his role. But then, like Albert, he too seems to be a man of riddles.

On Sunday 28 March, Mimi visits Albert at Mercer Street.

After they've enjoyed discussing the musical evening, she tells him that she has an idea for a school project with photographs: 'Dr Albert Einstein'.

'Will you co-operate?'

'Yes, by all means,' Albert says with enthusiasm. 'Ask me questions.'

'May I begin with your family?' Mimi asks.

Albert fills his pipe and lights it. 'Yes. Yes. I have lots of family photographs. A photograph never grows old. You and I change. People change but a photograph always remains the same. How nice to look at a photograph of Mother and Father taken many years ago. You see them as you remember them. But as people live on, they change completely. That's why I think a photograph can be kind.'

'I think so too.'

They sit side by side at his desk. Albert produces albums of family photographs.

Mimi takes notes and with her Ansco Shur-Flash box camera takes a selection of photographs of the family pictures in Einstein's albums.

'My father was Hermann Einstein. German-Jewish. Born in 1847. He died in 1902.'

'What did he do?'

'Do? He was a featherbed salesman.' Einstein shows Mimi some sepia-toned photographs. 'As a child, of four or five years, my father showed me a compass. The needle behaved in such a determined way, a way that was all out of place concerning the manner of the events that could find a place in the unconscious vocabulary of concepts . . . I still remember today . . . the experience left a permanent impression with me.' He sighs. 'He had two children with my mother, Pauline. Me and my sister, Maja. Maja died in 1951.'

'Who's this?' Mimi asks.

'Mileva, who I married in 1903. We had three children. One, Lieserl Marie, is no more. We had two sons, Hans Einstein born in Bern, and Eduard Einstein, born in Zürich, who was institutionalised for schizophrenia. Milena and I divorced in 1919 and the same year I married Elsa Einstein-Löwenthal, my cousin, who had two children by her first husband Max Löwenthal. I inherited two stepdaughters, Margot and Ilse. I have a grandson, the son of Hans Albert, who is Bernhard Einstein; and Klaus, who died of diphtheria as a child, and a granddaughter, the adopted daughter of Hans. And so, that's my family. Simple, isn't it?'

'Not really,' says Mimi. 'I want to talk to Dr Oppenheimer.'

'You do – why?'

'I want to know about your role in the production of the atomic bomb.'

Albert flinches. 'My role in the production of the atom bomb consisted in a single act: I signed a letter to President Roosevelt. This letter stressed the necessity of large-scale experimentation to ascertain the possibility of producing an atom bomb. Oppenheimer will tell you I was well aware of the dreadful danger for all mankind, if these experiments would succeed. But the probability that the Germans might work on that very problem with good chance of success prompted me to take that step. I didn't see any other way out, although I always was a convinced pacifist. To kill in war time, it seems to me, is in no way better than common murder.'

'Is that still your judgement?'

'Of course. Remember this, Mimi. The most beautiful and profound emotion we can experience is the sensation of the mystical.'

He points to the framed emblem of the Jain religion, symbol of the doctrine of non-violence.

'The hand is open. In the position of the *abhayamudra*, see, the Hindu and Buddhist gesture? The wheel in the centre is the wheel of Samsara, the law of *dharmachakra*. The word in the centre of the wheel reads *ahimsa*, without harm. No violence. All of us are together on this small Earth, yet each person thinks that he's at the centre of it. We exist in parallel lines, yet we meet, don't we? We meet in space-time. It's a matter of relativity, Mimi.'

'$E = mc^2$?'

'Yes – I have talked long enough. I want you and Isabella to come sailing with me. You will enjoy yourselves. So will I.'

TINEF

Later in March, Albert takes *Tinef* out with Mimi and Isabella on the windswept Mercer County reservoir, Lake Carnegie.

He hands Mimi a pencil and a pad of paper. 'Hold these in case calculation is required.'

He takes advantage of the wind, oblivious to the choppy water and the spray. Mimi and Isabella sit on the floor of the boat either side of the centreboard, resting their backs against the seat.

'Think of Melville,' Albert calls. "Consider the subtleness of the sea; how its most dreaded creatures glide under water, unapparent for the most part, and treacherously hidden beneath the loveliest tints of azure . . . Consider all this; and then turn to this green, gentle, and most docile earth; consider them both, the sea and the land; and do you not find a strange analogy to something in yourself?"'

Mimi and Isabella hold on tight to the sides of the little boat. Albert knows what he's doing. Whether he can actually do it is a different matter. The spray drenches all three of them.

'Our progress relies upon our direction relative to that of the wind. We can't sail directly into the wind. But with the wind at forty-five degrees we'll make a tack upwind.'

Tinef hurtles across the water. Fearless, his pipe jammed in his mouth, Albert as helmsman is indifferent to the passing sailing boats whose helmsmen shout warnings. Albert calls out to them: '"Vanity of vanities; all is vanity."'

With increasing consternation Mimi and Isabella notice that Albert's hands are shaking and that he's shivering violently.

'Would you like me to take the tiller?' Mimi asks.

'If you like,' Albert says.

'Sure,' says Mimi.

Mimi's taking over the tiller involves all three of them shifting places in the boat. The wind is buffeting it. All the surfaces are slippery. What would normally be a simple and swift manoeuvre is awkward. Isabella more or less stays put.

Albert manages to stand in a crouching position. He holds onto the tiller with one hand, reaching out for Mimi with his other to steady himself.

Isabella leans forward to give him support. In so doing she considerably alters the weight on board. The boat bounces and tilts.

Albert slews sideways, his twisting body causing the boat to tilt at an even steeper angle. He loses his balance, lets go of Mimi's hand, topples backwards out of the boat into the waves and disappears beneath the surface.

'Oh no!' Mimi howls.

To avoid striking the submerged Albert, she sails the boat away for three or four lengths, then executes a tight, fast gybe, lets the sail luff, sailing closer into the wind.

She steers the dinghy back to where she sees the distraught Albert has surfaced. Against the wind, she slows the boat, pushing the boom to leeward to reduce speed. The boat has almost stopped at the point where Einstein is next to it.

Mimi controls the boat's angle while Isabella reaches out over the side to grab Einstein's jacket. With all her strength she pulls him back on board, settling him on the boat's floor.

'We're going back,' Mimi calls against the wind.

Isabella cradles the bedraggled Albert in her arms, who says to her: '"I wish I hadn't cried so much!" said Alice, as she swam about, trying to find her way out. "I shall be punished for it now, I suppose, by being drowned in my own tears! That will be a queer thing, to be sure! However, everything is queer today."'

Albert's name opens many doors. Frau Dukas finds Bradley Beaufort's proves no exception.

It's 85°F and humid in the Washington neighbourhood known as Foggy Bottom. Beaufort's office is in the CIA building complex facing the US State Department at 2430 E Street NW. The CIA sign and seal are clear to see.

Beaufort greets Frau Dukas in his office with old-world courtesy.

'I appreciate your allowing me to visit you,' Frau Dukas says.

He asks her to explain her concerns and Frau Dukas tells him the story of the visit she'd received from the FBI agents.

A secretary takes notes in shorthand.

Beaufort opens various files on his desk. 'You understand, Frau Dukas, that the CIA is not the FBI?'

'I know,' she says.

'Dr Einstein's record is extraordinary,' says Beaufort. 'Scientist. Philosopher. Activist. Always an opponent of chauvinism and racism.'

'I know,' says Frau Dukas. 'He spoke out in defence of the Scottsboro Boys, victims of racism in Alabama, and after the lynchings in 1946 he joined Paul Robeson on the American Crusade Against Lynching.'

Beaufort opens another file. 'There is a view that he has Communist sympathies.'

'His defence of the Communist Party never implied support for Stalinism. He spoke out in defence of free speech. Please – is that a crime?'

'No, it isn't.'

'He never concerned himself with issues raised by the Russian Revolution.'

Beaufort looks at her directly. 'But he considers himself a socialist. Think of what he wrote in the *Monthly Review*. "The economic anarchy of capitalist society as it exists today is, in my opinion, the real source of the evil . . . I shall call 'workers' all those who do not share in the ownership of the means of production. In so far as the labor contract is 'free', what the worker receives is determined not by the real value of the goods he produces, but by his minimum needs and by the capitalists' requirement for labour power in relation to the number of workers competing for jobs."'

Frau Dukas scarcely contains her impatience. 'Please—' she says.

'Hear me out,' says Beaufort. '"Under existing conditions, private capitalists inevitably control, directly or indirectly, the main sources of information, press, radio and education. It is thus extremely difficult, and indeed in most cases quite impossible, for the individual citizen to come to objective conclusions and to make intelligent use of his political rights. Production is carried on for profit, not for use."'

'What do you mean by this?'

'He says . . . "In such an economy, the means of production are owned by society itself and are utilised in a planned fashion. A planned economy, which adjusts production to the needs of the community, would distribute the work to be done among all those able to work and would guarantee a livelihood to every man, woman and child."'

'Have you finished?' Frau Dukas asks.

'I have,' says Beaufort. 'But I'm merely repeating Dr Einstein's own words.'

'I know,' says Frau Dukas. 'He dictated that article to me.'

'So we must at least take a balanced view about the visit the FBI agents made to you.'

'If you say so.'

'I do say so.'

Frau Dukas gets up to depart.

'Wait, Frau Dukas,' Beaufort says.

He shows her a file marked: Federal Bureau of Investigation Freedom of Information/Privacy Acts Section. Subject: ALBERT EINSTEIN. File Number: 61-7099.

Beaufort hands it to the secretary. 'Show Frau Dukas to the exit,' he says. 'Then take that file to the furnace.'

'You want it destroyed, sir?' the secretary asks perplexed.

'That's what the furnace is for,' Beaufort tells her.

He smiles at Frau Dukas. 'The Director of the Federal Bureau of Investigation will doubtless keep a copy. Let him. As far as the United States government is concerned there will be no further investigation of Dr Einstein.'

'Is that really the case?' Frau Dukas says in a whisper.

'This morning I discussed the matter with the President. We find ourselves in complete agreement. Dwight Eisenhower is a man of his word. Now, Frau Dukas,' says Beaufort, 'be sure to give my love to Mimi and Isabella.'

'I will.'

'They're very talented musicians – remarkable young women.'

'I know,' Frau Dukas says. 'They think the world of Dr Einstein.

I suspect they're a little bit in love with him. And vice versa. Dr Einstein has always had an eye for the ladies.'

'So I gather. And the ladies for Dr Einstein. In any case, the free world owes him an incalculable debt. He's one of the greatest men who's ever lived.'

The telephone is ringing.

The secretary takes the call and stiffens. 'Sir?' she says. 'For you—'

Ever the compulsive eavesdropper, Frau Dukas lingers outside the door.

'Who is it?' she hears Beaufort ask his secretary.

'The President, sir,' the secretary says. 'He wants to know how the interview went.'

For the rest of 1954, taking care of himself is demonstrably what Albert fails to do.

That's the view of the dandified Dr János Plesch, who gives his patient a thorough examination.

Plesch asks Albert if he's suffering from pains in his chest and Albert says emphatically he isn't.

So Plesch has him strip to his underpants, lie down on the examination couch, sit up, and breathe deeply.

'My chest hurts,' says Albert 'Why does it hurt me?'

'Because there's a swelling of the fluid-filled sac surrounding this heart of yours. You have pericarditis.'

'I do?'

'Yes, you do.'

'Do I have to go into hospital?'

'No. You need good rest. A salt-free diet, and diuretics. And stop smoking your pipe.'

'Stop smoking my pipe?'

'I leave that up to you.'

233

'I can't stop smoking my pipe.'

'Think about it. I want you to take a few days' rest at home. No visitors. No work.'

'My liver hurts,' says Albert.

'Your liver's fine,' Plesch tells him. 'It's your heart that we must keep an eye on.'

Albert more or less takes his doctor's advice and conveys it to Frau Dukas. However, he's insistent it doesn't restrict him from taking calls from Mimi and Isabella, who tenderly wish him a speedy recovery.

The idea that the diminution of Albert's strength is the result of the incident on Lake Carnegie haunts Mimi.

'I'm sorry,' she says. 'It was my fault.'

'It was last year,' Albert says. 'It was no one's fault. Certainly not yours.'

'I was so fearful. It was a silly accident.'

'The fear of death is the most unjustified of all fears,' Albert tells her, 'for there's no risk of accident for someone who's dead. What more can I help you with, Mimi – your project – how is it progressing?'

'Just fine,' Mimi says. 'I wonder – only if you don't mind – could you ask Dr Oppenheimer if he'd spare a few moments to talk with me?'

Albert agrees to do so.

So Mimi calls Oppenheimer's office at the Institute. According to his secretary, it seems Oppenheimer's diary is full.

Familial duties interrupt the progress of Mimi's project.

Whitney Beaufort is fading and is taken into hospital.

Mimi and Isabella spend the long vacation at Beaufort Park.

Sometimes Mimi speaks to Albert by telephone and plays her violin for him. Mozart's Sonata for Violin in E minor, K.304. It becomes a kind of ritual. Some days Isabella does likewise.

Kurt Gödel keeps in touch with them. He tells them that Albert is missing their visits and is concerned about their welfare.

'He's asked me to keep an eye on you both,' Gödel says. 'He thinks you're fine musicians. So do I. Take my advice. Study and practise until you achieve perfection. Like Dr Einstein.'

In the autumn, the sisters' visits to Albert at Mercer Street resume and continue throughout the cold Princeton winter.

Albert delights in their music making.

Mimi begins a new commonplace book and enters lines from William Carlos Williams: 'The only thing left to believe in – someone who seems beautiful.'

And:

For Albert

bonfire smoke maple glow
bonfire burning leaves
needle-tip splash of scarlet oak
tulip poplar chrome yellow
hues of oak and hickory
ash mahogany rising mushroom colour
leaf gold of black hickory

Mimi Beaufort
1954

On Friday 17 December, a grey still day, Mimi, Isabella and Einstein at Mercer Street listen to the radio coverage of President Eisenhower switching on the lights of the Christmas tree in Washington, heralding the Christmas Pageant of Peace. Fifty-six smaller trees are illuminated, representing each of the fifty states, five United States territories and the District of Columbia.

The President says: 'Even at this happy season, we dare not forget crimes against justice, denial of mercy, violation of human dignity . . . Neither dare we forget our blessings.'

'You think all this will do America any good?' Mimi asks Albert.

'It won't hurt,' he says.

'What would you like for Christmas?' Isabella asks him.

'That new miniature radio I've seen advertised in the newspapers. The Regency TR-1 transistor radio.'

On Christmas Eve, Mimi and Isabella give him the Regency TR-1 transistor radio.

Albert gives them advance copies of his *Ideas and Opinions.*

Albert has inscribed each of them:

> Your idealism and music making have lighted me on my way, and time after time given me new courage to face life cheerfully. You demonstrate Truth, Goodness, and Beauty. Without the sense of fellowship with men of like mind, of preoccupation with the objective, the eternally unattainable in the field of art and scientific research, life would have seemed to me empty. You remind me of the beauty of Botticelli's Venus emerging from her shell. The reason you are beautiful is that, like Venus, you don't know it.

In the New Year of 1955, Dr Oppenheimer finally grants Mimi an interview.

He leads her graciously into his office at the Institute. There's a hat stand by the door with a pork-pie hat on it. Mimi gives it an admiring glance.

'I wore that at Los Alamos,' says Oppenheimer.

He's tall, ascetic, thin to the point of fragility, with a long nose and intense, vivid, blue, unsmiling, penetrating eyes.

He sits, chain-smoking and biting his fingernails, behind his desk beneath a large blackboard with a maze of equations chalked across it.

He fiddles with his blue shirt collar and suddenly, with his spindly arms, he lifts himself from his chair to pace rapidly and flat-footedly around the room.

He questions her briefly, with concern, about the sailing accident and asks tenderly after Einstein's wellbeing. It strikes Mimi as a little odd that he obviously hasn't telephoned Einstein to find out for himself.

She explains her high-school project to him.

'You don't mind if I ask you some questions?'

'You can ask me anything you wish,' he tells her with a smile of considerable charm.

Mimi prepares to take notes.

'What d'you have in common with Dr Einstein?' she begins.

'For a start, we're both children of non-observant Ashkenazi Jews.'

'D'you still do research into physics?'

'No. I'm the humble director of this Institute. Naturally I read the journals and follow what's happening in high-energy physics and quantum-field theory. Ignorance is the parent of fear.'

'You're an outsider like Dr Einstein?'

'Up to a point. You could say so. We belong to different generations, but yes – I suppose we've that in common.'

'You first met some twenty years ago?

'In 1932 at CalTech, the California Institute of Technology. We've really only established a close relationship in the last seven years or so since we became colleagues here at the Institute. He's been a great support to me.'

Oppenheimer breaks off. He makes curious noises, his strange conversational mannerisms, '*Nim-nim-nim-nim*' or '*hunh-hunh-hunh*'.

'You know the recent history of my security clearance suspension?'

'I know some of it.'

'Last year I was told my security clearance – that is, my access to secret information – *nim-nim-nim* – was being withdrawn, because of accusations that my loyalty was in doubt. I exerted my right to request proper hearings. Alas, they led to the cruelty of three weeks' quasi-judicial interrogation. Including, amongst other matters, questioning about my opposition to a crash programme for development of the hydrogen bomb and my contacts in the 1930s and 1940s with Communists. Dr Einstein spoke up on my behalf.'

'He said he admired you not only as a scientist but also as a great human being?'

'He did, yes. *Nim-nim-nim.* It was gracious of him. I've continued here as director and with my writing and lecturing. Sometimes audiences at my lectures give me ovations, y'know, in expression of their sympathy and their outrage at the treatment meted out to me. Even so, my ease, my peace of mind and my happiness has all but been destroyed.'

'Dr Einstein doesn't consider ease and happiness as ends in themselves. Like Schopenhauer.'

'I know that he believes that one of the strongest motives that lead men to art and science is escape from everyday life, with its painful cruelty and hopeless dreariness, from the fetters of one's own ever-shifting desires. I sympathise.'

'But isn't it true that for over two decades Dr Einstein has been isolated from the community of theoretical physicists?'

'Maybe that's true. But he remains a charismatic example to the world in so far as he represents the image of the great scientist. Perhaps the greatest the world has ever seen.'

'What are the differences between you, I mean, in terms of character traits?'

Oppenheimer smiles bleakly. 'I'm no Sigmund Freud. But, now you ask, I suppose clouds of myth surround him. He's wholly without sophistication, wholly without worldliness. In England people would say that he doesn't have much "background". In America the view is he doesn't have much education. He isn't even a very good violinist. He has no natural converse with statesmen and men of power. I do because I believe in the discipline of mind and body. *Hunh-hunh-hunh.* Discipline. Yes. Authority. Discipline.'

'And you perhaps defer to authority?'

'Yes.'

'Whereas Dr Einstein doesn't?'

Oppenheimer gives a wan smile. He lights another cigarette. 'You could say so.'

'Was that something for you that underpinned the invention of the bomb?'

'Let me tell you something. There's a line from the Hindu scripture, the *Bhagavad Gita*. This is what underlined the invention of the bomb. Vishnu trying to persuade the Prince that he should do his duty. To impress him he takes on his multi-armed form and he says, "Now, I am become Death, the destroyer of worlds." One way and another I guess we all thought that. You must understand that I selected the site for the creation of the atom bomb. By 1945 the high and lonely mesa was home to some four and a half thousand souls working on the bomb. All the main decisions were mine. They were all correct.'

'You were fearful?'

'Fearful of what?' Oppenheimer flicks the burning ash from his cigarette with his little finger. Mimi notices the callus the habit has caused.

She asks: 'Fearful that the bomb wouldn't work?'

'I feared what would happen if it didn't. Understand this. The bomb had to be made.'

'That's the truth?'

'It's hard to tell the truth in life. There are accidental truths. Sometimes truth happens in a way that is unexpected. You see, truth and falsehood sometimes get confused. But pure science and technology are complementary. Everything you find of quality turns up in a gadget someday. That's true quality.'

'What is Dr Einstein's quality – his fundamental quality – what lies at the centre of his heart?'

Oppenheimer draws deeply on his cigarette. 'Goodness and extraordinary originality,' he says. '*Nim-nim-nim* . . . intellectually, his understanding of what it means that no signal can travel faster than light. His brilliant understanding of physics. The general theory of relativity. His discovery that light would be deflected by gravity—'

He gazes into the distance.

'Just being with him is a wonder. He's a man of great goodwill towards humanity. How can I put it? It's a kind of harmlessness he evinces. In a word, the Sanskrit *ahinsa* – not to hurt, harmlessness. A wonderful purity – at once childlike and profoundly stubborn. Christians will say: Glory to God in the highest, and on Earth peace, goodwill toward men. As to the bomb and the equation . . . *hunh-hunh-hunh*. He wrote a letter to Roosevelt about atomic energy. I think this was to do with both his agony at the evil of the Nazis and then not wanting to harm anyone. But the letter had no effect. He's not answerable for all that came later. For Hiroshima – for Nagasaki.'

'Everyone thinks he is.'

'Maybe they do.'

'Are you answerable?'

'Maybe I am. *Nim-nim-nim*. Einstein himself knows he isn't. He isn't responsible for the supreme violence of atomic weapons. He discovered quanta: the profound understanding of what it means that no signal can travel faster than light. Even now, the general theory of relativity is not well proven. Only in the last decade can we fully praise Einstein's discovery. Namely, light is deflected by gravity.'

'Who in all history does he resemble?'

'Ecclesiastes.'

'Ecclesiastes?'

'Yes. He's the twentieth-century Ecclesiastes. The Hebrew Koheleth, gatherer, teacher, preacher, who tells us with his indomitable cheerfulness, "Vanity of vanities; all is vanity."'

'And you . . . father of the atomic bomb – why did you father the monster?'

241

'Because, when you see something that's technically sweet, you go ahead and do it and you argue about what to do about it only after you have had your technical success. That is the way it was with the atomic bomb.'

'Why was Nagasaki necessary?'

'To this day, I still don't understand why Nagasaki was necessary. Oh, yes, I know there are those who honestly think Japan had its fanatics refusing even after Hiroshima that it was time to surrender. The figures beggar belief. No one knows them exactly. I hear 140,000 perished at Hiroshima; 100,000 were terribly injured; 74,000 perished at Nagasaki; another 75,000 suffered from burns, injuries, and gamma radiation. The damage went deep into the bones. Everything between human skin and bone was instantly destroyed. Do you know what burning human flesh smells like?'

Mimi watches Oppenheimer light yet another cigarette.

He says: 'I hear there are people who genuinely think the wholesale destruction of the Nagasaki bombing and the butchery of men, women and children may have been performed to exercise the minds of the Soviets, a Cold War gesture. Well. Why not ask the children playing on the streets of Princeton for their view?'

'Do you really think they understand what happened?'

'Why shouldn't they? There are children who could solve some of my top problems in physics. You know why?'

'Tell me.'

'Because they know things I forgot long ago. Long ago.'

In February, Mimi asks to see Kurt Gödel.

They make an appointment for Thursday 3 February, which turns out to be the coldest day of the year in New Jersey, with a low of 1.4°F.

It's Gödel's idea that they meet in Albert's office at the Institute.

242

Equations cover the blackboard. Books are stacked on the shelves in no particular order. Einstein's chair is at a sideways angle to the desk.

It's an odd encounter. Mimi, in full bloom wearing an ankle-length cashmere coat with a wide lamb-fur collar and Gaylees fur-trimmed snow boots, stands facing the skeletal Gödel and vice versa.

Gödel removes his scarf and overcoat.

'He understands the universe in its entirety,' he says, peering at Mimi through his round glasses. 'He has a set of principles that cover everything. He is near to God. He understands by thinking. Thinking. Thinking. A thousand times I have heard him say: "I will have a little think." I am a being of numbers, of abstractions and shapes that have no existence in what's called the real world. Think of a number. What is it?'

'Ten.'

'Ten what?'

'My ten fingers.'

'You can see your ten fingers. But you cannot see ten. You cannot *see* the shapes of geometry. You see a picture of a triangle, say. It is not a triangle. They do not exist on this Earth. They exist in your mind. Think of time. Think hard.'

'I am thinking hard.'

'Good. You see? It doesn't exist.'

Mimi senses that Gödel's mind is wandering. Suddenly he says: 'You've talked to Oppenheimer?'

'Yes.'

'What did you think of him?'

'He's cold. Distant. But very courteous.'

'He's too concerned with politics in Washington. He's burned out. Unlike Einstein. There are a few words in Goethe's epilogue to Schiller's *Song of the Bell* could've been written for him: "The thoughts that were his own peculiar birth; / He gleams like some departing meteor bright, / Combining, with his own, eternal light." I fear for him. On the 14 March he'll be a remarkable seventy-six years old. He's so frail. He's weakening—'

Like an almost sightless man, Gödel peers around Einstein's office, his arms flailing like the wings of an emaciated bird.

'He'll never see this place again. This place will never see him again. "Doubt thou the stars are fire. / Doubt that the sun doth move. / Doubt truth to be a liar. / But never doubt I love."'

Gödel leans against the wall in despair. 'What will I do with my life . . . what will you do with yours – what is your dream?'

'I had a dream,' says Mimi, 'a dream to study music in London with my sister. At the Royal Academy of Music. But our family doesn't have the money to pay the tuition fees and expenses. The dream has ended.'

'I'm very sad to hear that,' Gödel says. 'Be bold. The Almighty may provide.'

'I wish I could believe it.'

'The more I think about language,' Gödel says, 'the more it amazes me that people ever understand each other at all. But never give up hope – d'you feel the cold?'

'Yes.'

'We have that in common. Alas, "Crabbed age and youth cannot live together—" You know who wrote that?'

'Shakespeare, I think.'

'In fact it's unknown,' Gödel says. '"Youth is full of pleasance, / Age is full of care; / Youth like summer morn, / Age like winter weather; / Youth like summer brave, / Age like winter bare."'

He smiles at Mimi. 'Believe in the mysterious and magic. Remember Goethe. "Magic is believing in yourself, if you can do that, you can make anything happen." Albert has it right. "The most beautiful thing we can experience is the mysterious. It is the source of all true art and science." Don't forget.'

In mid-March, Frau Dukas telephones Mimi and Isabella at their lodgings.

'Dr Einstein asks that you visit him,' she says. Her voice verges on the distraught. 'He wants you two to play for him Mozart's Sonata for Violin in E minor, K.304. Kurt Gödel will be here.'

Mimi and Isabella arrive at Mercer Street and find Frau Dukas to be more cheerful than she'd sounded on the telephone.

Albert is delighted to see them.

'Look,' he says. 'An Englishman, a physicist at Princeton, has sent me this for my seventy-sixth birthday.'

The gift is a contraption consisting of a five-foot-tall rod. A small plastic sphere is attached to one end, penetrated by a tube. There's a small ball at the end of the tube.

'This is a model to demonstrate the principle of equivalence. The string with the ball is connected to a spring. The spring tugs and tugs at the ball. Look, it can't manage to conquer the force of gravity tugging at the ball.'

Albert pushes the rod up and the sphere almost reaches the ceiling.

'When I allow it to drop there will be no force of gravity. Now the ball will enter the tube. Watch!'

He allows the contraption to drop until it touches the floor. And the ball nestles in the tube.

'Hey presto,' he laughs and the others laugh with him. 'You remember . . . I told you about seventy years ago my father gave me a magnetic compass. I owe everything to that compass.'

'No matter you twisted it here and there trying to outwit it,' says Mimi, 'to get the arrow to point in a new direction. The needle always went round to point to magnetic north. It demonstrated that there is something behind everything, something hidden in the universe.'

'Yes. Yes. "Come out," I would whisper,' Albert says. '"Where are you hiding?"'

Mimi and Isabella look at him with love in their eyes.

They've heard the story of the compass before. And Mimi, of course, has memorised it.

Now they feel an acute sense of joy, for in Mimi's violin case is the special present they've bought for him.

They intend to present it to him after they've played the Mozart.

'Now,' says Albert, 'to Mozart—'

'Mimi, Isabella – help me downstairs. Frau Dukas – where's Gödel?'

'He's on his way,' Frau Dukas says.

Mimi and Isabella support him by his arms and help him negotiate his way downstairs to the music room.

Frau Dukas answers the door to Gödel.

'Ah, Kurt,' says Albert, 'my spindle-shanked demigod. The greatest logician since Aristotle.'

Gödel frowns. 'You can't prove it.'

'I have just dictated a letter to Posterity,' Albert announces. 'Please read it to us, Johanna.'

Fantova leafs through her shorthand pad and reads the letter aloud: '"Dear Posterity, If you have not become more just, more peaceful, and generally more rational than we are. Or were. Why, then, the Devil take you. Having, with all respect, given utterance to this pious wish, I am. Or was. Yours, Albert Einstein."'

In the music room, Mimi and Isabella play Mozart's Sonata for Violin in E minor, K.304.

Albert calls out: 'Bravo, bravo, bravo.'

'Thank you,' Mimi says. 'We have a little surprise for you.'

'Mimi and Isabella,' Albert says. 'Before you two surprise me yet again . . . Please. In all the time we have enjoyed our loving friendship, neither of you has ever once called me Albert. Please. Call me Albert.'

The sisters smile into his eyes and Albert smiles into theirs.

Together they hold out a small package tied with ribbons.

'For dearest Albert,' says Mimi. 'Here's an object made by the British firm J.M. Glauser & Sons.'

'This,' says Isabella, 'is a Mark 4, with the ability to trap bubbles in a double casing before the liquid is topped up.'

'Is it a British bubble-making machine?' Albert asks.

The sisters laugh.

Mimi tells him: 'Similar items were provided for the Mount Everest expeditions in 1922.'

'And again in 1924,' Isabella adds. 'This is a bit more modern.'

Albert unwraps the package, which contains a pristine Glauser Mark 4 prismatic compass.

'I will call this beautiful creature "Mimi and Isabella".'

Early in April, Frau Dukas telephones.

A family problem necessitates her spending the night away from Mercer Street in Manhattan. Johanna Fantova is out of town. Would Mimi and Isabella watch over Dr Einstein for twenty-four hours? They're happy to agree.

They make him fettuccine and serve it, as he requests, with olive oil.

Later they tuck him up in bed, settling his head gently on the pillows.

Together they keep vigil by his bedside. Only the hourly chiming of the grandfather clock and Albert's occasional sighs interrupt the silence.

Albert's doctors find he has suffered internal bleeding, the result of an abdominal aortic aneurysm.

The doctors say that a surgeon might very well be able to repair the aorta.

'I want to go when I want,' Albert tells them. 'It is tasteless to prolong life artificially. I have done my share, it is time to go. I will do it elegantly.'

Albert dies at 1.15 a.m. on 18 April 1955 in Princeton Hospital. He's seventy-six years old.

President Eisenhower says: 'No other man contributed so much to the vast expansion of twentieth-century knowledge. Yet no other man was more modest in the possession of the power that is knowledge, more sure that power without wisdom is deadly. To all who live in the nuclear

248

age, Albert Einstein exemplified the mighty creative ability of the individual in a free society.'

For Mimi and Isabella the New Jersey spring at Beaufort Park is as sad as it is beautiful.

They find the loss of Albert almost unendurable.

They pin newspaper and magazine photographs of him on their bedroom walls.

Isabella practises Mozart without cease.

Mimi passes the time writing *Dr Albert Einstein*, and reading as many of his works as she can obtain.

She invests in a Smith-Corona Skyriter portable typewriter, along with the 'Smith-Corona 10 Day Touch Typing Course' on long-playing gramophone records. Isabella joins in the instruction and helps Mimi with the typing.

They wish they could have shown the pages to its subject.

The sisters' future is bleak.

They've learned that there are no funds available to meet the

Royal Academy of Music's tuition fees, travel and accommodation expenses.

Downcast, they return to Beaufort Park to face the uncertain years that lie ahead.

On Wednesday 22 June, the mailman delivers an envelope to the sisters. It contains an invitation from Kurt Gödel to accompany him to the movies. Gödel's chosen film is Walt Disney's *Lady and the Tramp*.

Along with Gödel's invitation is a letter addressed to them marked 'Private & Confidential'.

To: Miss Mimi Beaufort and Miss Isabella Beaufort
From: Dr Otto Nathan, Attorney-at-Law
Executor: The Estate of Dr Albert Einstein.
Co-Executor: Miss Helen Dukas

In the matter of the Estate of Dr Albert Einstein

I am directed to inform you that the late Dr Albert Einstein of Princeton, New Jersey, wished that financial considerations would in no circumstances prevent you from pursuing your studies at the Royal Academy of Music, Marylebone Road, London NW1, United Kingdom.

My firm is instructed to pay your tuition fees and necessary travel and accommodation expenses in full. Dr Einstein wished you to know, in his own words:

'I wish you every good fortune in your life. May God watch over you. I hope somewhere in the universe I may do likewise. I will do my best.'

A black-and-white photograph is enclosed.

It is inscribed:

> For Mimi and Isabella Beaufort
> Albert Einstein Speaking

IMAGE CREDITS

TEXT CREDITS

Every effort has been made to trace copyright holders and obtain their permission for the use of copyright material. The publisher apologises for any errors or omissions and would be grateful if notified of any corrections that should be incorporated in future reprints or editions of this book.

We are grateful to the following for permission to reproduce copyright material:

Extracts from *Born-Einstein Letters, 1916–1955*, by Albert Einstein & Max Born, Macmillan, 1971. Reproduced by permission of Macmillan Publishers Ltd.

An extract from a letter from Arnold Sommerfeld to Hendrik Antoon Lorentz on 24 April 1912, published in *Paul Ehrenfest: The Making of a Theoretical Physicist* ed. M.J. Kein, p.185, published by Elsevier Science 1970.

An excerpt from the poem 'St. Francis Einstein of the Daffodils' by William Carlos Williams, from *The Collected Poems: Volume I, 1909–1939,*

ALBERT EINSTEIN (1879–1955) was born in Germany and died in the United States. He was a world-renowned physicist who received the Nobel Prize in 1921 and, the same year, was made a Fellow of the Royal Society. An icon of the twentieth century, his is still one of the most recognised faces in the world.

MIMI BEAUFORT was born in Greenwich, Fairfield County, Connecticut. Her family name means 'beautiful fortress' and she grew up in The Fort, within her family estate of Beaufort Park, Greenwich. She and her younger sister, Isabella Beaufort, attended St. David's College in Princeton where both girls excelled in the study of music.